Black Cat's Tales

Liam Ó Murchú had a varied and successful career as a public servant, broadcaster and writer. He continues to enjoy literature, music, swimming and hurling, and is the author of the bestselling *Black Cat in the Window*, the first in the *Black Cat* trilogy.

Black Cat's Tales

Liam Ó Murchú

The Collins Press

Published in 2000 by
The Collins Press,
West Link Park,
Doughcloyne,
Wilton,
Cork

British Library Cataloguing in Publication data.

Printed in Ireland by Betaprint

Typesetting by Red Barn Publishing

ISBN: 1-898256-34-9

Contents

Preface

'When all our worldly goods are piled high on
the dray, I am plonked up beside them – the rest
of the family can walk. Off we go then, like
those share-cropping prospectors in the American mid-west, hungry to inhabit our new-found
world. From my perch aloft, I look back upon
the house where I was born. There is a black cat
in the window – a sign of luck? But is the luck
before us or behind?'

So ends the first chapter of my recent memoir, *Black Cat
in the Window*. The stories in Part 1 here come from the
same time in my early life and are woven from the same
thread: little Ben Buckley praying to his 'Special Agent' for
a miracle to save him from the shame of his patched backside in the big Corpus Christi procession is no different
from the ragamuffin 'Dear Johnny' who auctions the goodies his widowed mother has given him so that she will not
go short. Here, too, are the soldiers and sailors, still han-
kering after old glories, but back now to a life in the alleys
and back-lanes, where love and loathing live side by side –
as they do in the final story 'Honour Thy Father', when
young Terence comes to realise, too little and too late, the
love he has for that crippled and embittered old man.

In Part 2, 'Later Tales', the pinchpenny world of slums
and lanes is left behind for the improver world of
white-collar moralities and the self-righteous people who

inhabit it. Here are the anonymous guardians of the public weal, who work like ants in an 'Anthill' and will take no rest until 'A Feast of Tap-Mites' stops them. But here too are the innocents abroad, like the young widower for whom his dead wife's sister becomes aware too late of 'The Hidden Spring'; and the first cousins within 'the forbidden degrees of relationship', for whom 'The Moons of Jupiter' light the way to a lifelong, unmarried love.

Some of the stories here were broadcast on BBC or RTE Radio, or were published in newspapers and magazines in Ireland, Britain and the U.S.

Special Agent

Aunt Agatha wasn't a bit like my other aunts – shell-shocked Mamie whose husband had been sent home from the Somme; stiletto-heeled Maggie over from London; and Aunt Nonie, the fattest woman in the world. They were all good, kind-hearted women who would give you the coat off their back if you needed it. What's worse, Agatha had a lot more than any of them, with her stiff and starchy husband, a foreman in the Ford Motor Works in Cork who neither drank nor smoked but spent his time in and out of churches, praying for the good of his soul. Small wonder, when Mother sent me to her looking for the loan of twenty pounds, that I should be the one who was doing the praying – praying for a miracle! 'I wish we had your Aunt's fat ould stocking,' Mother was saying as she sent me off. But even at that age it had not escaped my attention that people with 'fat ould stockings' had them because they never put a penny astray. If I never knew it, I would come to know it now.

She had seen that ragged old tracksuit on me day in day out for the past year, with the big brown patch in

1

the backside. How could I come out in front of everyone at the annual Corpus Christi procession through the streets of the city looking like that? And this year more than ever because the headmaster, Brother Enright, had decided that the first four in the Christian Doctrine test were to be out front carrying the school banners? Too bad for me, I had the misfortune to be one. But how could I, dressed up like a rag doll? Thousands of people would be lining the streets, watching me go by with my banner aloft and that big brown patch sticking out like a beacon in a bog.

'Look, look, there's young Buckley with the school banner . . . Look at his technicolour arse!'

How could I live with that? How could you? How could anyone?

Aunt Agatha had her answer: I had a father and mother of my own, why couldn't they see to me?

But it didn't need me to tell her that that Saturday would be the same as every Saturday, with me and Mother sitting in the kitchen waiting for Dad to come home, our ears cocked to the sound of every step, hoping the next one would be his. His dinner would have gone cold and stiff in the pot and the little islands of dripping in the onion soup would still be there, hard and untouched, when I came down on Sunday morning.

Mother was never done finding excuses for him being late, all sorts of weird and unlikely excuses – like that he was on overtime, or there was a strike or a train crash, anything and everything but the one thing which she knew as well as I did. If I went up to bed and left her there, I knew I'd be woken by the sound of her sobbing and Dad's voice rising above it, angry and thick with drink and heavy with menace. And I'd know then it wasn't me she was fooling at all but herself.

So she gives me the twenty pence for my bus fare and sends me on the beggar's errand. Knowing Aunt Agatha as

I did, I think I knew even then it would come to nothing; but beggars can't be choosers. Besides, I had this wild hope, something Mother was always saying to us when we were in trouble – friend of the poor when he was on earth and still friend to them when he's in heaven, somebody called 'Saint Anthony'. There's this plaster statue to him in the Holy Trinity Church and there are always people going in, women mostly, lighting candles to him in the hope that he'll act as go-between for them with God the Father to get them whatever it is they want. Up to this, I never wanted much but, even if I did, I couldn't see how lighting a candle to this Saint Anthony could help me get it. But Mother was a great one for the praying and, I suppose, if you want something bad enough, you might as well believe in Saint Anthony or anyone else to get it for you, if it will do the trick. Even while I'm thinking this, though, I'm also thinking that this holy guy, whoever he is, is going to have his work cut out getting skinflint Agatha to loan us the price of a new outfit and save me from the shame of that patched backside tomorrow. As you can see, I'm all mixed up inside about this – yet what other choice have I but to go?

'Saint Anthony is our special agent inside the gates of heaven,' Mother says, as if people can have special agents in heaven. 'Go over to your Aunt and ask her. And say a little prayer to him on the way.'

I do more than say a prayer, I go into the Holy Trinity and drop the twenty pence she gave me for my bus fare into the poor box under his statue. It's not much for what I'm asking but it's all I have. Then, I light a candle and leave it lighting, in the hope that it will keep jogging his memory as I go on my way.

My aunt is alone in the house when I go in. She is polishing the hall floor and barely nods to me. At the first sight of her, I recall that she is famous in the family for fainting, a thought that scares the living daylights out of me. What if she faints when I drop the bombshell that I am looking for the loan of twenty pounds? I'm the only one there, how will I bring her around? Maybe she'll never come around, just lie there dead as a dodo on the ground, because the shock of what I said or did killed her?

'Twenty pounds?' she shrieks. 'Twenty? Are you gone soft in the head, boy? The cheek, the nerve of some people!'

She has this habit of letting several little yelps out of her like a trapped dog when something bad happens, yelps that can turn you inside out with terror when you're not expecting them. Should I run for it while I'm still to the good? Saint Anthony won't be anywhere near to stand up for me, if she ups and dies. He'll say what everyone else will say – that it was I who killed her; which in its way will be true enough. Then I'm in real trouble, and all alone in it, Saint Anthony and all that lot being at a fine, safe remove.

Yet, what else can I do but stay? Stay and hope and – do what Mother does – pray? It is Saturday and soon the shops will be shut. Then, there will be no way I can get a new outfit, and nothing will stand between me and the shame of that patched backside tomorrow.

Agatha did not die. But I could have wished that I did. I remember, with the pain of a thing you don't want to remember but cannot forget, how she picked up the polishing cloth she was using and shook it out until the air about me was thick with dust. I should have known then what was coming.

'Your mother must think we're made of money,' she said. 'Go back home and tell her I said we could all be short of cash if our menfolk drank it.'

Sometimes a thing happens and at the time it hurts but, later, when you look back, you can laugh at it. This was not one of those times. Even still, I can feel the stab of realising that what was all the world to me was nothing at all to someone else; and the feeling of being alone that comes with it. I hated my Dad for his drinking that made us poor; and I hated being poor for forcing me onto my knees before someone who knew only how to hurt me for it. And, once and for all time, I knew that nothing, not even the shame of my patched backside, is ever worth selling your pride for.

I felt another thing too, something that no amount of the silly excuses Mother would think up for him when Dad was on one of his drinking bouts could ever start up in me. This was something to do with Dad himself. Once, long ago, I had been trick-acting with the sweeping brush, trying to balance it on my forehead like I had seen the clown do in Duffy's Circus. Dad was sitting at the table nearby reading the *Evening Echo* but, with all my attention on the brush, I hadn't noticed him. Then, suddenly, I lost control and down it comes, smack on the side of his head. Blood began to spurt and run all over his face. I could see him wince with the stab of pain and I shut my eyes, expecting him to jump up and belt me.

But he doesn't. And, when I open my eyes to see why, it is to find that it is Mother who is in the rage and about to belt me and he, with his free hand, is holding her back.

'Leave the child alone,' he says. 'He was only playing, he didn't mean to do any harm.'

And I, part in terror, part in grief, run away from them and off to bed, where I cry myself to sleep – because I had hurt him and, in return, he is good and kind to me?

Now, all that comes back to me; and I know, no matter how much he drinks, or how much he squanders what little we have, above all, no matter how much my aunt may try to blacken him in my eyes because of it – none of these things will ever blacken him for me or make me turn against him. He is my Dad and I love him. And, so far as I am concerned, he is and always will be the best Dad in the whole wide world.

So I leave Aunt Agatha's house, my last hope now gone.
With a heavy heart I'm on my way back home when I pass
the Holy Trinity Church. Well now, I think bleakly, I wonder what our 'special agent' has to say about this? I must
have been crying – who wouldn't in my place? – because
some women in the porch as I go in begin to cluck their
tongues in sympathy. Let them cluck, I think – in Agatha's
place, they would probably have done the same. I have a
drunk for a father, why should I cry when somebody plain-
ly tells me so? Inside, it is dark and cool and very quiet. At
the Saint Anthony altar, a few candles send up flickers of
weak white light. For a moment, my hopes flicker up with
them – it isn't Sunday yet, there is still time. But no, there
is not. Agatha has refused, by now the shops are shut.
Worst of all, the candle I had lit with my twenty pence has
gone out. It has been squashed down into its socket by
someone else with a petition to make. I hope they do better than I did, I bitterly think. So much for Mother's 'special agent inside the gates of heaven', who always gets
things for people who need them. Yeah, sure – provided
they have someone who cares for them and has the money
to pay! I blow hard at the newly-lit candle and its flame
shivers as it goes out. I should be sorry but I am not. Saint
Anthony and all that stuff is a lot of silly old cod. No fear
I'll ever waste another twenty pence on him!

So what is to become of me now? What is the point of hur-
rying home, there is nothing or no one there to help me. All
I have to say is that my aunt did not give me the money
and tomorrow I will have to act sick or dead or something,
anything but not be there.

But how can I not be there? It is going to be the biggest
day of my life. Already, all along the quays, procession
flags and bunting are strung out across the roadway; and,
in the little side-streets, it looks as if a million coloured
birds have been let loose and are going wild with delight

6

in the clear blue sky. There's this specially-made High Altar with a giant picture of the Last Supper above it; and up and down the steps on all sides of it there are billowing cascades of plants and flowers. Petals blow like snowflakes across the road and pile thick and high against the edges of the footpaths . . . Already, I am there! I can see myself and hear the whispers from people in the crowd who know me.

'Look, look, there's Ben Buckley out in front. He's carryin' the school banner.' Tattered rag doll and all as I am, how can I possibly stay away? Is there nowhere in that great crowd where a small boy can hide and yet be seen, have the honour and glory of it – and yet, when they catch sight of his rag-doll backside, not have the deep stabs of shame that will cut him through?

I look up at the giant picture of Jesus and the Last Supper and a swift, desperate surge of hope rises up in me. Saint Anthony, special agent and friend of the poor, has let me down. But this is supposed to be the Lord of the Poor, is He going to do the same? How can He let a thing like this happen when He is supposed to have the power to change it?

When I get home, one look is enough to let Mother know the answer I have got.

'Never mind,' she says, 'God is good. You'll see, Saint Anthony won't let us down.'

I'm never cross with Mother – you'd catch the wrong side of her if you were! – but I'm cross with her now.

'Don't be saying silly things like that,' I tell her. 'Saint Anthony, whoever he is, has nothing to do with it. He doesn't care about us and our troubles.'

'Never mind,' she says. 'We've been in worse scrapes than this and we came through. Anyway, it's not Sunday yet.'

'But it is. It's Saturday night and the shops are all shut. There's nothing to be done now.'

'There is,' she says mysteriously. 'Take off that gear and give it here to me.'

She sounds so sure that, for a moment, I think she is the miracle worker, a fairy godmother with a magic wand to turn Cinderella's rags into a glittering ball gown. But all she does is roll up her sleeves and throw the ragged track suit into the washtub.

'That won't do anything,' I protest. 'Washing won't change the colour of the patch.'

'Never mind the patch. First, we'll make it clean, we'll think about the patch later. Anyway, it's behind.'

Why this should make any difference is a mystery to me, but I do as she says anyway. I sit on the edge of the table in a tattered old jersey and pants of my Dad's. And, somehow, as I sit there watching her, half of my troubles drop away. It's something to do with the strong surge of her arms in the sudsy water and the bright bubbles rising up from it, as she kneads and pounds on the thick, grimy cloth. And I think how it will be when I grow up and have a job and money of my own and be able to buy her a new coat and a fox fur to go with it and a brand new clock for the mantelpiece which, as far back as I can remember, has only the one-legged alarm clock which is always stopped. I suppose that, in a way, is what makes mothers – the hundreds and hundreds of small things they're always doing for you, like the millions of raindrops that go to make a mighty river.

Before going off to bed that night, I look down at the clothes line in the back yard. There it is, my Corpus Christi dress wear, hanging out to dry. It is limp, sodden, threadbare – and it has the big brown patch sticking out of the backside. Well, I think, Saint Anthony can try for all he's worth and I wish him luck. But, if he can make decent gear of that, he sure deserves his title of 'miracle worker'.

Clean, spotless, the ragged edges all trimmed away, in the morning it is there beside me, on a hanger down at the bed-end. If I had been having a good dream about it, the reality could not have been better. My shoes underneath, newly-polished, are shining like prize apples. And there is a pair of brand-new socks, the limit of Mother's Saturday purse.

It is a miracle! I jump out of bed and put them on. In the cracked mirror of the wardrobe, it looks perfect. God, God, can it be true? In my sleep, has our 'special agent' been busy? I stand there staring at myself, afraid to turn around. When I do, my heart sinks. There, still, is the big brown patch. It comes screaming out at me, bigger and browner than ever.

God, Saint Anthony, the whole shebang of you in heaven and earth, I have news for you: there are no such things as miracles or, if there are, they don't happen to poor little scrubbers like me. There are far too many people in the world who are crippled or blind or have nothing to eat for God and his saints to be worrying about a small boy with a patch in his pants afraid of being laughed at. I heartily wished I could be struck by lightning or that the ground would open up and swallow me, like it did with the poor people in the earthquake. Then I would have a fine, dramatic excuse for not turning up at the procession at all. But it's a bright blue day out there, with hardly a cloud in the sky. And there's not a sign of an earthquake anywhere.

If only things could be changed around a bit: if only it would rain today rather than last Sunday when the big match was on and nobody wanted it; if only my Dad had the will to say 'No' more often and my Aunt Agatha the will to say 'Yes'; if only I myself had not been so bloody smart as to get that place of honour with the banner out front where everyone would see me; or if that big mouth of a Headmaster hadn't come to the school that very year, with his bright ideas for filling the front row with smart guys instead of fellas with new suits. If, if, if . . .

But it was no use, it was all stupid make-believe. For, already, I have the banner, its pole slippery from the cold sweat breaking out on my hands. I cling tight as ivy to the school wall, with the front of me showing. Left and right of me are the other banner bearers, Collins and Dempsey, and beyond them the new boy, Wheeler. They're all out in spanking new gear which their mothers bought for them yesterday. They look like something straight out of airtight cellophane packets. It is less than five minutes until the procession forms up and I am out there in front with them. What can happen in five minutes? New clothes, no more than new pennies, do not fall from heaven.

The Headmaster arrives, walks up and down between the lines, surveying us with what looks like a critical eye. Can it be that he has already spotted me and is thinking of some nice polite way to send me packing?

'You four with the banners,' he says, 'come over here.' Lightly, with that same critical look, he touches us on the shoulders, one by one.

'You fellows look like shop models. I just want you to know, and I want your parents to know, that this is a Corpus Christi procession, a procession in honour of Our Lord in the Blessed Sacrament. It is not a fashion show or a mutual admiration society.'

There is a cardboard box on the window ledge beside him, long and flat, like the ones you see in classy women's shops. He goes over and opens it. Inside, the tissue paper cover comes away with the lid and floats limply to the ground.

'Here,' he says, 'put these on.'

I take mine. It is a long red cassock with a white surplice to go over it.

'These are all I could lay my hands on in a hurry. In my last school, I made it a rule every boy should wear one of these on church occasions like this. Next year, please God, we'll do the same here.'

I shove my head through the neck and feel the silky cloth slide down over me like a light, feathery sleep. I put the white surplice on over that. All four of us, the three 'shop models' and me, are now dressed the same, front and back. All that stands out between us are my bright new socks and my shoes shining like prize apples.

Birds of a Feather

1 – Unwilling Partner

A whole world apart in nature and in temperament from my Aunt Agatha was my Uncle Timmy. She was always making herself busy, constantly gossiping and gabbling, mostly berating neighbours and relations about things that didn't matter; while he was a quiet, silent man, the short pipe permanently clenched between his teeth – which meant that, even when he did speak, we could barely make out what he was saying. He had been shell-shocked in the First World War and left for dead by the German guns amid the blood and mud of Flanders. When, eventually, a scouting party picked him up and carried him off with them, he did not know who or where he was and ended up in a prisoner-of-war camp behind the lines, where he was locked up for the duration, half-starved by all means but still safe and sound, until the war was over.

When he was released, he came back home but, little as he knew about where he was when he was shell-shocked, he seemed to know even less now. So much so that the only thing he was at home with were the birds chirping on the eaves and, even more than them, the ones he kept in the birdloft jammed up against the wall in the backyard of his little moss-lined home. This was on Drummy's Lawn off Shandon Street in the city of Cork in the south of Ireland. For Timmy, it could have been anywhere in the whole wide world.

The birdloft he kept beautifully painted in black and white and always immaculately clean. So far as I was concerned, what he had in there were birds of paradise, with the constant chirping and chattering and the dazzle of wings as they went trapezing wildly all over the place. He would see me there looking in at them and, little as he seemed to be aware of anyone else in the world, he was well aware of me. It wouldn't have been hard for him to guess that I would have given my eyes to have a bird of my own, not one of the lovely technicolour ones he had – canaries and finches and cockatoos – but just an ordinary, everyday bird, a linnet, a sparrow, a black-bird, a thrush, anything so long as he would be my own, to perch on a swing in his cage from morning till night, piping his heart out to get me up and admire him or, more likely, to fetch him fresh water and birdseed to fill his hungry little gut. Oh, yes, I'd be man and master of him by all means; but I'd still have to hop and jump to his every whim and wish. None of this would I mind a bit, so long as he was mine – to have and to hold for all time and eternity! Yes, I was small; yes, I was only ten; yes, the grown-ups around me were always telling me that small boys should be seen and not heard. But he wouldn't think that.

For him, I would be the giant in the story, Gulliver, with my big, battering-ram fingers pushing the gate of his

Lilliput cage aside and my blue eyes blinking in at him as he fluttered about, trying to placate me.

But what was all this only daydreaming? I didn't even have a bird, not to mind a birdcage – and here I am already making plans for him! Last Christmas Mother, in a crazy moment, bought me a goldfish in a bowl; and fine and exciting that was until, one night, when we were all fast asleep, Chublo the cat jumped up and pawed him out and gobbled him, smashing the bowl in smithereens on the ground; which, of course, had Mother swearing blue murder on any of us who ever dared bring another pet into the house.

But faith can move mountains – or is it hope? One day, when I'm looking in at this birdloft of my Uncle Timmy's, he comes up behind me and taps me on the shoulder.

'You're fond of the ould birds, boy?' he says.

'Indeed I am, I just love looking at them.'

'Very well then, I'll tell you what we'll do. I'll knock up a birdcage for you, if you'll go out to Lane's Wood and catch a fledgling for yourself to put in it. How would you fancy that now?' Oh, I'd fancy it fine and well the ould codger knew it. But was he serious about the cage? One with slim bars all around it, a swing where the bird could bounce and do somersaults for all he was worth, and a sliding panel where I could push the birdseed and the eggcup of water in? Yes, he was: in the long days and months and years he spent in the prison camp in Germany long ago, some of them used to pass the time doing little handcraft jobs like this. But, even if he did, how would I face Mother when I brought it home? Especially after the row she kicked up when Chublo gobbled old Goldie, having smashed his shining bowl?

As for getting the fledgling, that would be the least of my problems. Hadn't me and Danny Joe and Pa Connors several nests out in Lane's Wood where, at that very time, the eggs were hatching; when the fledglings came out, any of them would do. So, I forget clean about Mother, Chublo, Goldie and all that. This is it, this is going to be a real personal pet, one I had found myself, and would feed and water myself, someone my very own! A right pair we'd make in time, with him hopping and bobbing and chirping all over the place and playing blue hell with the laws of gravity in Uncle Timmy's specially-constructed cage; and me sitting there looking at him, admiring him, as he goes on with his acrobatics before my very eyes! As you can see, this was going to be the best-bred bird that ever had the good fortune to be caught.

He would have such a time of it that, later on, if I happened to leave the cage panel open and he got out, he'd hop right back in again, without any hint or help from me, remembering the small nibbles there would be for him out in the great wide world – compared to the fine, toothsome titbits he got served up daily by me. Out in the wood where his brothers and sisters were, he was just one in a million; in here with me, he would be a very special bird, a personal mascot and pal of mine, a double act all of our own.

For this, he would have to have a name. I fix on 'Gerry': it's a nice perky little name, a bird's name, but a homely kind of a name as well. I'd have this special whistle for him too which, when he'd hear it, he'd pop onto the swing and cock his head and look at me, with the eyes blinking, as much as to say – 'Well, what do you want Gerry to do for you now?' Oh, a very clever little lad this is going to be, I'm going to teach him just about everything.

But first I have to catch him. It's well into May now and all the birds of the air are up in the branches, chirping and chattering and singing their heads off – like when Mother goes down to the launderette and all the neighbourhood women are there, yapping away about the trials and tribulations their children are bringing on them. But those birds are no use to me. They're too big, too feathered, too cute to be caught. Better stick with the nests I know and the fledglings there who will fly the coop as soon as they can.

Crossing the marshlands coming up to Lane's Wood, I hear a sudden panicky 'tweek-tweek', as up out of the spikey rushes a skylark jumps, spurting abuse at me. For a moment I am tempted to fall for the trick and follow her; but then I remember that skylarks are smart little gets and always do that – run under cover of the grass from the nest and only then take to the air, so no intruder will ever know where the nest is. But I can't be bothered with her tricks and head on for one of my own nests. It is evening, getting on for dusk; the moths are out and the corncrakes are squawking away in the marshes. I creep up and look in. It's a thrush's, a little brown bowl of a thing, hairy on the inside like the shell of a coconut, bedded firmly in a fork between branches. I stumble a bit on the way and get scratched by briars and brambles; the noise of me trampling the twigs and leaves frightens the mother bird, who flies up in a panic to the tree-top and now watches fearfully for what the intruder is about to do.

The intruder stands there above her nest, peering in. It's a whole world of wonder in there: the four fledglings jostling and pushing each other about, yet never too hard or too far because this is their home and there is room for them all in it. But I am the stranger, the odd man out. I touch them with the tips of my fingers; they are still warm from the sitting bird. Above me, a rapid bubble of sound gutters out – an alarm signal from herself perched away up there at the top of the tree. I do not like her being there and wish she would fly away. She does not fly away, she stays, uttering strange urgent little yelps and gulps which seem to be telling me something but I am not taking it in. What has her worried? What has her distressed? Won't her chicks be gone from her soon enough? Does she not know that all I am doing is finding a good home for one of them? What is here for them but the cold and leaky woods where all sorts of dreadful things can happen? In a snug cage at home with me, the one I take will be fed, watered and looked after just as well as any of the lovely fancy birds in Uncle Timmy's birdloft. What can possibly be wrong with that?

Still, I decide to wait a few more days until they are just about ready to fly. Each day, I go out to see how they are coming along; and each time I can see their independence day drawing closer. Their sticky pelts begin to be covered in a light crew-cut down, fattening up into little mufflers about their scrawny necks.

So I pick out what looks to be the biggest and strongest of them, an avaricious little fellow who is always up first with the beak wide open to catch whatever God may send him. On the way home, I hold him tightly in my hand and feel his tiny pulse against my palm. Every now and then, he peeks out gingerly between my fingers and I, for fear of harming him or of losing him, I know not which, tighten my grip to make sure he won't get away. All I know is that I do not want him to get away. Before all the other birds of the air, he is the one I want. He, and he alone, is – Gerry.

Uncle Timmy might have warned me about this but he didn't. With all the birds he had, and all the handling he had done on them, he must have known what happens when you hold a bird too tight. If he had given me even a hint, I might have brought the cage with me and not held him in my hand at all. But Timmy didn't and I didn't know any better – so what's the good of the 'ifs' and 'buts' and 'maybes' and 'might-have-beens.'

Gerry, my special bird, was special now only in one way: he did not want to be held by me. He did not want to be locked up in any cage, no matter how good I tried to make life for him there. That he made plain from the very start. He flung himself a dozen times against the bars when I put him in and then fell back into the corner, exhausted. His wings were all askew, his speckled brown-and-white breast was throbbing, his eyes opened and shut as if he was biding his time for a fresh assault. I went away and left him, hoping he might get used to it. He did not get used to it. This was not his home, the things about him were not his things, there was nothing or no one here that was like his place in Lane's Wood. I suppose that shouldn't have surprised me, but it did. Isn't it what I myself would have done if I were in his place? Didn't I act up all the time with Mam and Dad when I didn't get my way? Wasn't it cat-and-dog between my big brothers and sisters and me when things were bad? Yet, take me away from them and put me down in some strange place on my own and I wouldn't live a day. Wilful, headstrong, stubborn as a mule – oh, if you had a tune to it, you could sing it. We were a pair, Gerry and me, I could see that. That's why I wouldn't let him go; that's why he didn't want to stay. As it turned out, neither of us got our way in the end.

Later on, when I came back to him, he was still there, still hunched and huddled in the corner. And there, in the few days that were left, he stayed, refusing all the titbits I brought him – the breadcrumbs, the groundsel seed, the worms I dug up in the garden: all the things Uncle Timmy told me, hoping he'd stretch up and open his beak as he always did when his mother brought him things out in the wood. At ten, I don't suppose you can know much about broken hearts, but somehow I knew then that that was what was wrong. And, if it was, sure as hell I had no idea how to mend it. Anyway, one morning a few days later, I came downstairs to see how he was getting on – and found him dead.

Out on the lilac and holly trees in the garden and up on the powerlines shining in the sun, all the other birds of the air were going wild with delight. And here was Gerry, my special bird, tumbled to one side on the floor of his cage, his beak shut, his eyes staring in defiance at his too-greedy Gulliver.

Just then, it might have been nice to think – as some saying has it – that 'there is a special providence in the fall of a sparrow'. And nicer still to know what the providence was – though knowing the end before you know the means may not always be the best thing.

It's odd to think, though, that what must surely be the great mystery of life and death may have been at work there in a tiny birdcage on a bright May morning long ago, when there was no one there to see it but a fledgling thrush – and me. If there is such a providence, part of its goodness must surely be that it can waste its time on such unlikely things. Though perhaps not quite waste. For me at least, 'the fall of a sparrow' did this much: it taught me to live a little more by my heart: to be, if you like, a bit more of a fool than is commonly thought decent. That way, you get to love things more and, even if in the process you sometimes get hurt, sometimes too you can end up a little bit more happy.

All I hope is that Gerry, my special 'sparrow', did not think it too high a price to pay.

2 – *Partner in Solitude*

Uncle Timmy's birdloft in the backyard of his house on Drummy's Lawn did not long outlast my own brief time with 'Gerry'. Maybe it was the shellshock of the war years that did it; or maybe he was just getting old anyway; but he began to have these fits of forgetfulness, when he would sit out on a wicker chair in the yard admiring the technicolour capers of his finches and canaries, after he had finished feeding and watering them. The neighbours, not seeing him coming to the front door, as he always did when the bells of Shandon rang out at Angelus time, suspected that something might be amiss. They were right. One evening, when they went in, there he was out in the yard, slumped in the chair fast asleep, or so it seemed – until they looked again and saw that his eyes were wide open. When this happened a second and a third time, they put it to him as gently as possible that he could no longer look after himself as well as all the birds; so, one by one, he gave them away, to friends, neighbours and other bird fanciers, until only one was left – and that wasn't one of the smart, technicolour set at all, but a linnet.

How he came to have this bird in the first place is a story in itself. Some time before, in one of those fits of forgetfulness of his, he had left one of the seed-and-water slides in the birdloft open and the linnet, spotting the goodies within, hopped in and showed no sign of wanting to leave. So, having come into Timmy's life of his own free will, a total stranger amongst the others, the old man felt he should keep him. Bit by bit, a special relationship grew between them; so much so that, when all the others were gone, he had this one personal pal to keep him company.

The house itself was a warm, dried-up little place like the inside of a nut, with the plaster flaking from the walls and the flower-patterned paper above the fireplace gone stiff and brittle from the constant heat coming up from below. Every crack and splinter of it he knew as well as he knew himself; why wouldn't he – except for that time when he was away at the war long ago, he had lived there every day of his life. Down at the entrance to Drummy's Lawn at the foot of Shandon Street, right there in the middle was this granite column with flecks of silvery stuff like stars shining through it; it had been put there away back in the old gods' time to stop stray horses from the nearby stables wandering in and out. There were no horses now anymore, the stables were long since gone, and in their place was a bright new supermarket and car-park.

The dome of this column was round like a mushroom and polished smooth from the generations of kids who had gone up and down the lane and vaulted over it as they went past. Timmy, in his time, had been one of them; with his brothers and sisters he had gone up and down, vaulting over the column as he passed. But now they were all gone; some were dead, others married and settled in England and the States. So, from time to time when he came up the lane to the dark empty house, he would touch the mushroomed top with the tips of his fingers, and a whole world of memories and lost but not forgotten faces would come before his eyes.

In winter, the light went early and he would sit at the fire, with an old grey blanket about his knees and the ticking of the clock for company, dreaming the long hours of darkness away into the murmuring embers. What thoughts might have come to him then, what was his company in the dimly-lit room, nobody would ever know. In the streets beyond, life went on as it had always done, people laughed and cried, worked and worried, and in the big shining world beyond the lane the wheels of fortune and misfortune kept turning. But nothing showed from Uncle Timmy's house but a slit of light from under the door and, above, a plume of smoke rising from the blackened chimney.

Now, suddenly, he had this new interest, this tiny creature who had come uninvited into his life when all the other birds were gone; soon they became great friends. The bird-cage he had made for my 'Gerry', I brought back to him and, all day long, with its new occupant, it would hang from a hook under the low eave just beside the door. There,

21

he could look out and watch it and hear it chattering and chirping to the other birds in the free air beyond. Sometimes, when there were lots of them about, it would go wild with excitement, flying from side to side of the cage like a demented thing, battering the bars with its tiny wings. At such times, looking at him, I couldn't help thinking of 'Gerry', locked up in this very same cage, where he didn't want to be, when all the other birds of the air were free. But what about the old man himself? Wasn't he a captive too? Why couldn't they both be happy, both making a life for each other?

That must have been very much in my Uncle Timmy's mind: if he gave the linnet its freedom and let it go, what would become of him, how could he get on without it? How could he stand the emptiness and the silence, which was full of chirping and chattering and the fluttering of wings while his partner in solitude was there?

If he went for a walk, which he seldom did now, his first anxious glance when he came around the corner from Shandon Street into Drummy's Lawn would be towards the cage hanging from its hook under the eaves. Good, it was there! His heart would give a little jump of delight then and on he'd come, his step quickening as he passed the granite column, never once looking at it or giving it a thought anymore.

At night, when he brought the cage indoors, he would put in fresh water and seed and, while he was doing so, out the linnet would pop, to make a great panic of wings and chirps about the room. He would pretend not to notice, just sit there on the wicker chair and wait. Soon, the panic would die down, there would be a little new fluttering every now and again, then total silence. The next thing, it would perch on the back of his chair right behind his head. Then, sure enough – pop! – it was onto the peak of his cap, its featherweight pressing down on his forehead, its tiny claws hooked over the rim.

'A smart little bugger you are,' he'd chuckle. 'Knows what's good for you, so you do!'

For that, it would get an extra cup of groundsel seed. Oh yes, the partners in solitude were getting to know each other's ways alright!

So the days and nights passed, the big brawling days of spring, the heavy days and nights of summer, and the little house was a happy house and Timmy was a happy man because now, for the first time in a long while, he had something of his very own to love.

Then one evening, when he was taking the cage down from the hook to bring it indoors for the night, the chair he was standing on slipped from under him and down he came with a thud to the ground. The neighbours heard it and out they came but, by the time they got to him, he was lying unconscious on the cobblestones, with that same dead look in his eyes he had when they found him in the backyard a while before. Wisps of white hair trailed across his forehead, his mouth hung open, show-ing his strong pipe-stained teeth. There beside him was the cage, its sliding panel open, the bird gone. Up on the roofs and wires, hundreds of linnets were chattering and gossiping in the last of the evening sun. No one, not even Uncle Timmy if he could see, would be able to tell which of them was his.

An ambulance was called and, as it pulled in at the end of the lane, his eyes flickered open and he looked about him at the upside-down world.

'What's up with me?' he stammered. 'Where am I?'

He tried to lift his head but it wouldn't come up and he fell back exhausted. The neighbouring women were down on their knees, holding him up by the shoulders and mak-ing soft comforting sounds like mother hens about a clutch of chickens: 'Hush, hush, Timmy boy', 'You took a little turn, you'll be alright'. One of the men took off his coat, folded it and put it under his head, so he could lie back. Some of them got between him and the cage to prevent him seeing it.

'Take it easy, you're with your own, we'll see you right. Just for safety sake, we're taking you up to the North Infirmary.' That set his mind at ease: it was right beside him, right under Shandon, where anyone who was ever sick or ailing about the place was looked after, a nice homely hospital where the neighbours could drop in to see how he was coming along whenever they were passing; hearing it, the ghost of a smile moved over his face.

'Me poor father and mother died in the North Infirmary,' he said slyly. 'Ye're not going to let the same happen to me?'

'Divil the fear of it, you're as strong as an ox, you'll be back out to us in a few days.'

'Alright so, ye can take me. But before I go, I want ye to promise me one thing.'

'What's that? Whatever you ask, we'll do.'

'When I'm gone, ye won't forget to water the linnet?'

The last of the evening sun was stretching long shadows across the roofs of Drummy's Lawn as the ambulance men lifted the stretcher bearing his body down; a few minutes later and it would come around to fling a golden shaft across the front of his house, where a rusty hook hung from the eaves and an empty birdcage lay sideways against the peeling wall. The bells of Shandon were ringing, they were playing the old airs he had listened to ever since he was a boy: 'Oft in the stilly night', 'Believe me if all those endearing young charms', 'The bluebells of Scotland'. The neighbouring women about the place who knew him in the old days blessed themselves and whispered a prayer as the stretcher went past; the menfolk stood in the doorways, silent, listening to the rise and fall of the sound of the bells and the drumming of the ambulance men's heels on the moss-lined cobblestones. At last, they reached the end of the lane, where the granite column stood in the way. They lifted the stretcher shoulder high in order to get past. Its sagging centre touched just once upon the polished dome; then it was gone.

The Orchard

My big sister Lil and I used to have this dream; not an ordinary dream, about ghosts or fairies or your leaden feet being stuck to the ground when the devil was after you – no, this was a real dream, something that could and would happen in the big bright world known as 'being grown up'. We were going to have jobs, get rich and then, then at last, we would have enough money to buy an apple tree for the back garden.

You have to get this dream into perspective: to us, an apple tree in the garden was the top of the pile, the very peak and pinnacle of respectability. If you had an apple tree, you *were* someone, you had money, you had status to go with the money; in a word, you were a member of the upper class. Certainly, you would no longer have to scrape and scrabble for cheap apples in the market place; you would have apples to your beck and call whenever you wished. Out the Black Ash near where we lived, there was this apple tree behind the wall of a big house, with the branches hanging out over the roadway. One day, when no one was looking, Lil hefted me up and I snapped off a twig, which we planted in a corner of our garden at home. There, we said to ourselves, we've done it: this time next spring, that will have taken root; a few years later and it will be in full and fruitful life. Then, we can have apples to our hearts' content for the rest of our life.

But the ice and frost of the black months cared little for us and our downy dreams. Come Easter the following year, and it was down to a withered, shrivelled up spike. We pulled it up in a rage and flung it away and swore we would never eat another apple the longest day we lived. Thank God the rage didn't last.

It didn't have to. Out the Black Ash there were lots of orchards, big and small and medium-sized, they were all over the place. Some of them sold apples when the season was in. No sooner would we see the notices chalked on the gates, 'Apples For Sale', than off home we'd go, bearing tidings of great joy.

'They're great big eating and cooking apples,' we'd tell our mother. 'You could make jam and apple tarts and apple jelly with them, and they're only ten pence the dozen – can we have that please?' Ten pence mightn't seem much, but to us it could mean the difference between going without sugar in your tea or butter on your bread for a week. We knew all that; knew too that we would have to walk to school to save the busfare; we wouldn't ask for a penny for the pictures for a month. Anything, anything at all, only please could we have that ten pence now?

Somehow, by some trick-o'-the-loop of our mother's budgetary magic, we usually could. What we didn't know then, but came to know later, was that for Mother – who could be as cross as a bag of cats when she wanted but could be an old softie at other times – giving was always easier than refusing.

Anyway, we soon got a liking for this one special orchard. It was big compared to some of the others about the place;

it was away from the farm of which it was a part. But, glory of glories, it had an apple loft. This meant that it was a classy place, one that was in the apple business in a serious way. Picture our surprise then when, day after day, when we came to the gate with 'Apples For Sale' chalked up on it, there it was locked and bolted and without a sign of life about anywhere. To say the least, it did not seem much of a way to go about selling apples.

After repeated noisy assaults by boots and shoes on the shattered woodwork, footsteps would start up far back on the gravel path inside; the slow, unhurried steps of someone who, whatever else was on their mind, was not in too great a rush to please the customers. This was the sign for the whole crowd of us gathered there, Lil and me included, to crush together to be first to get through the wicket gate, once the bolt was drawn. Then, in we'd go in a mad stampede along the path and up the steps to the apple loft.

At last, we were there! An Aladdin's Cave of a place it was; or maybe more like that scary place in the coloured comics, Hades – with us, the pale ghosts, standing at the ready for Charon, the boatman, to ferry us across the river Styx.

Charon was a woman. She was tall, gaunt and queenly; she wore a mossy pudding-bowl hat on her grey plaited head. One by one, she would take the baskets from us and we would lean across the barrier as she went off to fill them. There's usually a mob of us there but such is the silence that we can hear each other breathing. The least sound might break the spell and she might begin to count the apples instead of just loading them in . . . I see it now as if it was in front of me: the mounds of apples spilling out over the broken floor: russets and ambers, green of the whitethorn, pink of the pippin, all caught in a grimy grey light from the cobwebbed windows; the woman moving about in the half darkness; and us, with our eyes, our watching, wishing, hand-me-down-the-moon eyes, peering in from beyond the barrier, hoping, praying that this was going to be our lucky day.

From down below at the foot of the stairs, we could hear the others who had got their stash gloating over their good luck.

'How many did you get?'

'How did you do?'

'Look, I got more!'

Then, to a chorus of high-pitched whistling:

'Jeez, boy, I wish I was you. You're dosed with luck today!'

At last, it came to our turn. Lil hands in the basket and the woman goes back into the shadows. We peer after her, watching her every move. Suddenly, there is this sound, like the low rumble of distant thunder . . . If you throw an apple up, it comes down; but here, if one apple slips, the whole mound comes tumbling. Could it be our luck? But what luck can there be with only ten pence to pay for it? Yet it is true. One apple at the bottom of the pile slips and the whole mound comes with it. They will only get in the way if she leaves them; so in they go, the whole lot. Our basket bulges, Lil's shoulder hangs to one side like a scarecrow as we make our way down the wooden steps to bring our swag of fortune home.

Sometimes the store in the loft is low and off down the orchard we troop to pick the apples ourselves; though 'troop' is hardly the word, as we slink along behind our 'follow-my-leader'. She herself has never told us this, but there are rumours that there are great watchdogs in there, Alsatians and Dobermans, ready to leap out and devour any strangers who come raiding. Masses of chickweed and robin-run-the-hedge are fattening all over the place; they could easily be lurking in there. Apples, last year's, the year's before, the year's before that again, are sunken deep and rotten into the ground. Why has no one ever collected them? Is it because of the dogs that no one dared? There are lots of good, clean apples in there right now, what other reason can there possibly be? We follow our leader closely, itchy fingers daring, yet not daring, just in case those rumours might be true.

If we had dared, we would have had a surprise coming. For how could we, at the age we then were, have understood that there were no watchdogs in there for the good and simple reason that there was nothing in there to watch? This was a falling house, with nothing but the 'relics of old decency' about it, the rotten apples of a dozen years as well as much else. There had been a time when it was a thriving place, the sole supplier to all the big fruit shops in town; but it stood still in its supremacy, while the new era of the supermarket and the multinationals moved in.

Those were people with small time for old friends and old loyalties, buyers who shrugged off the pledges made to suppliers in the good old days as so much sentimental cod amongst a bunch of has-beens and old fogies. No doubt they were smarter, they knew all about cut-price and credits and the hundred and one other tricks of the marketing trade. So it was that it was the lady of the house herself who came along to serve our tenpenny needs, not some hired hand taken on out of charity for a few hours' work a day. It would have been a poor charity indeed if they were depending on us.

All this happened a long time ago. These days, when I look in at the fruit shop windows and see their boxes of apples from foreign parts nestling in wrappers of fine tissue – and at such fine prices too – I cannot help thinking of that woman in the orchard sending us home with our baskets laden, all for the tenpences we could afford. To her, down on her luck, it probably made the difference between that and nothing; although there might just have been a bit more to it than that.

Yes, her place had seen better times, the walls were crumbling, the ivy and weeds had run wild. She herself was old, in a little while she would not be worried about ivy or walls or apples any longer. When that time came, maybe it would not have been the least of her consolations that, while she could, she gave with both hands and added that mite to our children's world that, with nothing but a tenpenny piece, it would have been very hard to buy.

For the first time in years, Lil and I passed the place again the other day. The big gate is a lot more shattered now, with only a few blistered dried-up paint-patches to fight a rearguard action against the summer sun. In that fleeting moment, I caught a glimpse of us as we were then, a snapshot of a waif in short pants and his big sister in a flowery dress. Was that really us, a pair of lost, wide-eyed urchins, with all our ragamuffin pals about us, living in the sweet, sultry unconsciousness of childhood? Right then, I don't suppose we thought it would ever end, that it would go on like that forever and ever, the eternity of the living present, rich in innocent oblivion. By the time we could afford to have an apple tree in our back garden, we had long since given up wanting one. Life is a bit of a cheat like that. I don't suppose it will ever change now.

Still, other things have come along, other orchards, other apple trees. Young or old, unless you're a saint or a fool, you go on dreaming, handing in your basket and your ten pence, which is all your wits can rise to, hoping it will come out full to the brim. Sometimes, it does, mostly it doesn't. It's nothing then but the big grey gate shut in your face and, inside, the golden apples of the sun rotting into the soft green ground.

No matter about all that. The past is fixed and nothing can change it. It was a smaller world then, a simpler world, a world where children were easily pleased and the things they wanted a lot cheaper to come by. For us, in our little unsung backwater beside the Tramore River in the Black Ash of Cork, it is not too fanciful to say that a handful of bluebells or wild irises pulled up in the marshes was all we needed to fill our world. Lacking all but the pennies we lived the closer to life. And life, like the woman in the orchard, though she may have had a thin purse, gave us many lovely things to remember.

'We're all goin' down to Yawl'

Out the Black Ash near Turner's Cross in the south side of Cork, there was this stream. It wasn't a big stream, or a deep one. Sometimes, when a dry summer spell came along, it was down to a mere trickle. But it had a touch of magic to it just the same, especially when the banks were white with daisies in the month of May and covered in fallen blossoms from the hawthorn bushes that spread along the way. It wasn't the daisies or the hawthorn blossoms that brought us there, but the fact that it was the nearest place where we could try to learn to swim.

With the fury of pyramid builders, we would set about damming it up to make a pool that would be deep enough: first, a wall of stones; then, between the stones, clods and sods packed tightly together so that nothing could get through. It was labour in vain: the following day, when we came back to inspect, the sods would be pulped to pieces and the stones gone; and there we would be, looking in at the reedy shadows, right back where we started.

In a fit of fury, we would capsize what was left of the dam, pushing stones and clods and sods into the water –

doing them no harm, but leaving us drenched and sodden with the brown mud.

What was to be done now, how could we ever become swimmers now? Where would we find a place to learn? And nowhere, nowhere at all was the answer – but that in a few weeks' time it would be high, seaside summer.

The 'Sea-Breeze Excursion' to Youghal – to us in Cork, it is not 'Ya-hal' but straight 'Yawl' – began in June. Every waif and stray from the streets and lanes who could not remember a line of poetry in school, if it was to save their lives, had no trouble at all remembering:

> Goodbye Mother, goodbye all,
> Goodbye Mother, we're all goin' down to Yawl

Out at the front door from the crack of dawn we'd be, looking up at the sky with the seasoned eye of the weather forecaster, praying to God to push the clouds away, at least for the length of this Sea-Breeze Excursion day. Hope, as always, springs eternal:

'Look, look, up there. There's a bit of blue coming through. It's goin' to be a scorcher, that's for sure.'

An odd time, it happened, luck was with us, the 'bit of blue' came through. Out on the horizon, the clouds could blubber and sulk for all they were worth; the sun God was on our side this day.

The Sea-Breeze Excursion drew out all our resources. Sometimes, the clanging and clattering puff-puff would sit down on the track for what felt like an eternity, while light showed red up ahead and we waited for that stretch of track to be cleared. There we were, sardined together in the smothering heat, with the chocolate melting and the clothes sticking to our backs, dreaming of the golden glories of Youghal Strand a million miles away. But, sooner or later, the hooter sounded, followed by an angry jolt – and we were on our way. Little Island, Carrigtwohill,

Midleton, Killeagh – for generations of us happy warriors out from the slums and ribbon rows of Cork, those are the names in our fairy tales; stranger, farther, more fabulous than the enchanted gardens of *Aladdin, Snow White* or *Ali Baba and the Forty Thieves*.

'Better to travel hopefully than to arrive': yes, surely – provided the arrival is not too long delayed. Youghal is only 30 odd miles from Cork; even with all the stopping and starting, it should not take forever. Sometimes, alas, it looked as if it would. But always, at last and blissfully, we did arrive; not before rounding the sloping shoulder of Clay Castle, as usual playing its dirty trick on us by hiding the sea from view until we were right there on top of it.

The first sign we got of this was the cheering from the carriages up front as it came into view: the miles and miles of golden sand stretching away off towards Ardmore; the 'bit of blue' now spread all the way out to the horizon; the great, crystal-crashing waves trawling their necklace of white foam along the seashore. Oh, bliss was it upon that dawn to be alive, but to be young was very heaven!

Doors flew open, bags and baskets were thrown out, the mystery was that no one was maimed or killed in the stampede to get off the train and down the platform to the exit gate. A primus stove got hooked in the luggage-rack and was yanked away, rack and all; a thermos flask fell and smashed in smithereens on the ground, to be kicked to one side and forgotten – some long-suffering mother's consolation-prize of a hot cup of tea later in the day.

Drop them, leave them, forget them, there is only one thing in the world now: get out through the station gate and be first up and over the curved seaside wall.

There, there at last it is – Youghal Strand in all its pride and glory! Its froth-lipped foam would soon be tickling our toes, while, out beyond, the power and passion of those mighty waves were building and breaking along its whole stupendous length.

Large as the strand is, at the start it looks as if every available inch of space has been taken. Have we come all this way to find ourselves out on the hard sand, still wet from the night tide? But Youghal Strand is not that patch of gritty silt beside that dammed-up stream in the Black Ash, and soon we manage to find our place in the sun. Once settled, the battle orders are given:

> 'Unpack the baskets.'
> 'Get out the grub.'
> 'Get the primus going.'
> 'Get the hell outa me way.'

The strong and choking fumes from primus and lit fires sting-blind the eyes; sandwiches burst at the seams but down they go, sand and all; lemonade and Tanora – Cork's own special brand of it – are gulped and guzzled as if they were nectar of the gods. Each and every item of this *haute cuisine* is a mouthful of immemorial delights; no meal before or since will ever be its equal.

We are Robinson Crusoe, every last man jack of us, up against it on our island in the sun, with no fancy frills or flounces, such as the later world will bring, to take the thrill out of it.

But the big challenge is to come. Ever since we first laid eyes on the place, those pounding waves do something to the pit of our stomach. Ignore them by all means, pretend they're not there or, even if they are, that they are not for swimming in. But, if I am going to be a swimmer – and we all surely are – then, sooner or later, I must brazen it out.

Legend has it that Father was a great swimmer in his day: in that Dublin Fusiliers Regimental Record Book of his at home, there is a certificate which says that he did a three-mile swim in Malta long ago; what is a fact – Mother and all the older relations actually saw it – is that, year after year, whenever he was at home, he did the annual Lee Swim, from Vincent's Bridge to Water Street.

And, since we're in Youghal, it always comes up when we're here; as far as Cable Island, which is away out there on the edge of the horizon.

Don't I want to do the same? Don't I want to be as good a swimmer as he? But how can I ever be, if I never get into anything deeper than that piddly dammed-up trickle in the Black Ash?

Down at the edge, white foam swirls and runs about my feet. With each step, the solid ground gets farther and farther away. Streaming sand races under me, my heels sink into it, pebbles gargle noisily in the shale, as the wave turns and draws me out. What if these are shifting sands? If so, I won't need to move at all, just stand there, sink and be swept away. And what about the fish? The whales, sharks, swordfish? Aren't they all out there, watching, waiting for this tasty morsel to come out to them? But there are hundreds, thousands of others about, they are in and out of the water up the whole mighty length of Youghal Strand. Surely all of them can't be wrong?

I take my courage in my hands and do what may fancifully be described as a dive. It is not a dive, it is a collapse. What is certain is that I am underneath something and it has to be water. But it isn't water, it is a thousand demons pummelling and pounding the daylights out of me. My head is where my heels should be and the rest of me is nowhere at all. For hours and hours, I am plunging wildly about, trying to gain a foothold on where the earth used to be, but I cannot because I am being strangled and manhandled by these giant new monsters coming at me all the time. My eyes shut tight, my hair streaming, salt brine stinging the life out of the place where my nose used to be – up at last I come, flailing the air about me. But, so far as I can judge, I am still alive and breathing.

Have I done it? Have I braved the sea and won? Yes, yes, the light from the Cable Island lighthouse winks at me, to confirm it. At long last, I am my father's son.

The long day closes. Soon, the sun is dropping down behind the hills away to the west. The tide is rising, slowly, steadily it fills the ribs between the sand. It is gathering, growing, sliding towards us like a dark shadow covering the strand. We scramble onto the curved sea wall and watch the waves come up to devour our place in the sun.

Soon now, it will be the same mad scramble back onto the homebound train, with shoes and socks, sandals and shirts, togs and towels sodden wet and thick with sand, all bundled together into the baskets and bags which are the lifeline of our sojourn in this, our home-grown Eden by the sea for one short summer day. The waves crash in about us, chafing our heels like a collie with a flock of sheep; up and over the wall we climb and onto the strand road. We hear the shrill whistle of the train above the slang of gulls screaming at us to get off to hell out of there and leave them to feast upon the scraps and pickings of the loaves and fishes with which we have enriched them in recompense for robbing them of the peace and quiet of *their* Youghal Strand for a whole long day.

Meanwhile, on the station platform, as we crush and crowd each other to get in, the regular holiday-makers leer mockingly at this unruly and chaotic mob – those grandees of Cork from the heights of Montenotte and St Luke's, who own or rent holiday homes all along the seafront.

'Oh no,' they seem to be saying, 'we are not like you. We do not have to rush back, we are staying down. Good to see you and all that, but only for the day, thanks. Because you are a scruffy lot, with your sausages and sandwiches, your Tanora, tarts and tea. Goodnight, goodbye, give our love to Cork. And don't be in any hurry back!'

The lullaby night comes down, the seabirds dive and rise above the swish and swallow of the waves. Out on the horizon the great arc of the Cable Island light sweeps like the wing of a guardian angel across our very own span of the broad Atlantic in the south-east corner of Cork. Children sore from sunburn and cranky with sleep bawl their way through the gathering dusk. A light breeze from the buttercup fields is rich with the scent of new-mown hay coming fresh and cool through the open carriage-windows as the first stars come out above Rostellan, Killeagh and Garryvoe. Young and old, we are children in a lost world and our one-day stay in the Arcadia of our dreams is at an end. Up ahead is bleak old Monday morning, awaiting us like a jailer at the terminus in Glanmire.

The city lights come on, dimpling the darkening night. A time will come when I am far from here, with a world of time and space between me and those beckoning lights, which we are now rapidly approaching. But that time is not now, it is away off in a dim and distant future, a future which knows nothing about us and the penny-dreadful wonders of our little day.

For Sea-Breeze Excursions come and go and Cable Islands always seem to be so far away. Maybe that is what dreams are all about: having big things to hope and plan for – and curse too when they do not come right? Yet, where are you, me, any of us, without them? And how poor a life it would be without the hope of that 'bit of blue' which made that Robinson Crusoe one-day stop of ours in Youghal a day to remember!

Don't Blow Your Trumpet

Millennia come and millennia go but who can boast he was there the day the world ended? I can. There was all the trembling and praying and penance you would expect to see for such an event and, to top it, the crowning glory – a sky to beat all skies, red and purple and burning gold, a sky that looked as if it was getting ready to fall down on top of us and hurl the whole lot into the fires of the last destruction.

Looking up at it, we knew for certain that something strange was going to happen. I was six, Lil and I were with the other kids playing on the steps outside our house in Goulnaspurra at the foot of Shandon Street and Blarney Street. The game we were playing consisted for the most part in being hauled by one of the big ones, like Lil or Nancy Tallon, down the steps on a coal sack. Not much of a game, not much of a place, certainly not the place you wanted to be when the end of the world caught up with you.

Sometimes, when the mood was on us, Lil and I would start dreaming up places where we would like to live, like the grand part of Sunday's Well or the golden mile out the Western Road, places that seemed heaven compared to our two-roomed tenement house. But no sooner did word come through that the world was going to end, and that big rotten old tenement of ours along with it, than I found myself looking at the windows four flights up, all red and glowing in the light, with Mother and Dad inside, and thinking: what's any place, even Sunday's Well or the Western Road, what's heaven itself – if it isn't going to be just like that?

But, like it or lump it, that's how it was going to be. By this time tomorrow, neither I nor it nor anything else would be here. We would all be blown to bits in the last great bang. Not that the idea of the end of the world was new to me; it was in fact one of the few things that stuck, whenever God and heaven and hell were talked about, which was a lot of the time. It would be started by a trumpet-blast from Michael the Archangel, which would wake the dead from their graves to join up with the rest of us who were still walking around. Then, we would all be lined up and trooped off together to the Valley of Jahosaphet for the general judgement by God the Father, surrounded by all the angels and saints. Down out of the sky they'd come, a mighty horde, far better than Ben Hur with the chariots or Yul Brynner with the Magnificent Seven. That, in a way, would make you kind of look forward to it: if it was going to be that good, the end of the world mightn't be a bad old number after all. But good or bad, we were to be given no choice. Lil's pal, Nancy Tallon, had spoken and that was the end of it. She was twelve, much the oldest of us; what's more, she could read and write – and never stopped boasting about it. Now, she stands there glaring at us, two red patches coming up on her fat little cheeks. She has just read the news in *The Echo*.

'Up to the North Cathedral with ye quick,' she says. 'An Indian prophet has announced that the world is going to end tonight.' We know that the Cathedral is for praying, and praying is what you must do to save your soul. We have no idea what a soul is and less still why you have to pray to save it; but Nancy Tallon says so – and Nancy is always right. So grim is the news she now brings that none of us for a second doubts it. Myself, all I can see are rockets and planets streaking the sky, all hell-bent on destroying whatever comes in their path. Our tenement house could easily get in the way; God help anyone who happens to be around when it starts flying. The hinges on the front door are thick with rust and the cast-iron knocker is big enough to brain an elephant. Where could you hide? With slates and doors and floorboards flying, you'd be sure to get hit. Unless you were in bed, safe, under the clothes, where even the headless monster couldn't get you. But the end-of-the-world monster would get you no matter where you were, under the clothes or over them.

So we do as Nancy Tallon says and head for the North Cathedral. Then, suddenly, we notice that a lot of people seem to be going the same way. Have they all read the piece about the Indian prophet in the *Echo*? Once in, they get down on their knees and start praying for all they're worth before the big bang comes. Better do the same and pray with them. I try but don't know how to start. It's my last chance, tomorrow will be too late. Yet all I can think is: please God, don't let it happen. Michael the Archangel, please don't blow your trumpet tonight. Save my soul by all means, if that will do you or me or anyone else any good, but think of some other way to do it, without having to blow up the whole world in the process. Slum-room tenement and all, I'd still prefer to be around, even if I got heaven on a plate instead tomorrow.

'Say an Act of Contrition quick,' Nancy Tallon snaps at me as she catches me looking around at all the ould ones with scrawny necks and ould fellas with shiny heads. 'Say you're sorry for your sins and that you'll never sin again.'

'How can I sin again when I won't be here?' I snap
back. 'Didn't you say the end of the world was tonight?'

'Shut up, don't be giving cheek to your elders. As you're
at it, you can tell God you're sorry for that.'

I do as she says. I tell God I'm sorry, though I don't
know what I'm supposed to be sorry for. Nancy is a right
bitch, that's one thing I'm sorry for; the reason I know
she's a bitch is that Lil calls her that whenever they fall out,
which is pretty often. I'm still kneeling there, petrified, not
able to put the words together, while the big door in the
porch keeps swinging open and shut, and more people
come in. By now, everyone has read the *Echo* and what the
prophet from India has said. Why couldn't the big eejit
keep his mouth shut? Or, if he had to blab, why couldn't
he blab to his own people out there and leave the rest of
us alone? Didn't he want to stay alive like us? Heaven can
be as grand and happy and beautiful as they say – but
thanks, no thanks, I'd just as soon stay where I am.

Besides, who was to say that it was heaven you'd end
up in and not the other place? What would happen if you
got mixed up, got in the wrong queue or something? The
thought of hell for all eternity, with Nancy Tallon's foxy
little eyes looking out at me everywhere, turned me inside
out. But, whether I liked it not, heaven or hell it was now
going to be.

I try again to say I'm sorry for my sins and the Act of Contrition bit – but it's no use. So I get up and leave and come
out on to the top of Shandon Street on my own. The red
sun is now down over the roofs on Blackpool and there are
great streamers of orange and yellow and silvery white
splashed across the sky. Oh, it's an end-of-the-world sky
alright. Out there from behind the hills above Gurrane
they'll come, the angels and archangels, the great big bossy
ones with wings stretching halfway to Dublin Hill; the
sugar-and-spice ones, cherubim and seraphim, names that

sound as if they came straight out of women's scents and toilet waters. There they'll be, sweeping down from Mayfield and Barrackton, on wings, in chariots – all with the same message: that the game is up and we're on our way. And then, at last, the trumpet blast of Michael the Archangel to blow us sky-high from the cobbled lanes and alleys of Cork into the parched sandy wastes of the Valley of Jahosaphet.

I see it and I run. Run where, you say? Where else but the place I want to be when the big bang comes – home. Dad is getting ready to go to work – he's on the night shift at the railway junction out in Kilbarry. There he is, sitting at the table finishing the last of his dinner. Everything looks as it always looked: his razor up beside the cracked mirror above the sink; the *Echo* in front of him, open at the racing page; his lunch box on a chair by the door where Mother always leaves it.

At long last, he folds over the *Echo*, takes off his glasses and gets up to go. I want to shout out at him that he's not to go, that he's to open the *Echo* again and find the place where the prophet from India says the world is going to end tonight. I want to tell him he's to stay at home with us, that I don't care about hell or heaven, or anywhere else for that matter, so long as he and Mother are still around to mind us.

'Dad, don't go out,' I finally let it out. 'Nancy Tallon says it's in the *Echo* that the world is going to end tonight.'

He doesn't answer, never so much as pauses or looks at me; just pulls the cap down over his eyes and draws open the door.

'Ah, sweet Jesus in heaven,' he says mysteriously, 'I only wish it would!'

Dear Johnny

Of the whole bunch of us who were out from Cork city on the Irish language *cúrsa* in Ballingeary, Johnny Farrell was the only real 'guttie' amongst us. Not that the rest of us were up to much – it was the year before I won my fine City Scholarship, which put me in the millionaire bracket compared to the others; but that was away off in the future, now we were all much the same – all, except Johnny. What with his crew cut, his slit eyes like a trapped animal, and the nicotine-stained fingertips, he had all the looks and manners of someone who had to rough it in the lanes and back alleys around the city centre Marsh.

There was a bakery on one side of the lane where he lived and a fruit-and-vegetable store on the other; both were familiar with the sight of Johnny going by, his slit eyes peeled for a chance to lift a slab of chester cake or a bag of apples from the front counters. Life was bad for him like that, but it was good too: the regular hunt for such bonanzas added zest and edge to what would otherwise be a very dull time. But now, he was free of all that; free to come and go as he pleased in the Gaeltacht above

Gougane Barra – which to be truthful, was about the last place on earth you would expect to find him. Still, he was a bright lad in his way and had no trouble convincing the people who sponsored boys to go out on the *cúrsa* that he would do well.

What a change it made to the place he had come from: when he looked out the window in the morning, there was the whole wide valley of the infant River Lee below him, with the sun's rays stretched like golden fingers across it – instead of being hemmed in, as he was used to seeing sunlight, between the bakery wall on one side and the peeling brick of old tenement houses on the other. Sometimes, passing the entrance to that lane where he lived off the North Main Street, we would see kids like Johnny standing with their backs to the bakery wall to take in some of the ovens' heat. Though he was often among them, he wasn't as ragtag and bobtail as most; though his Dad was dead, his mother – however she managed it – always saw to it that they were fairly well dressed, Johnny especially, who was the eldest and the apple of her eye. But now, for a brief spell, he was away from all that, out in the wide open country, as free as the birds of the air and, like the birds, he was going to enjoy it.

However, some of the rest of us were not. We were supposed to be learning Irish, which would help us at school later on and, hopefully, put us up a notch when exam time came around. Whatever that might mean – and it means little enough when you are twelve – there was not much else happening in the way of fun and games to keep our attention and fill the never-ending days.

We fished for trout or thorn eels in the stream at the foot of the glen; to the curses and pitchfork threats of the small farmers who were trying to build them, we slid down the sides of the haystacks in the fields; worse still, we parachute-jumped from the stacked hay in the barnyard to the ground level below. At night, the *fear a ti* –

man of the house – took us hunting rabbits in the moor grass or up on the hillside – a good game, only the rabbits were too smart and too fast and we couldn't catch up with them. So, by the end of the first week, all that had been tried and done and the novelty was gone. From then on, there was nothing to do but sit around, chasing beetles, pelting stray hens or ducks until the unlucky creatures took flight. At times like that, it seemed an eternity to us until the month was up and we could go back home; to all of us – except Johnny Farrell.

To him, only a fool and right eejit could feel bored as long as he had a few smokes to take his mind off it. He hadn't had a single smoke since the few bob his mother had given him before going away ran out. That was early on in the first week.

'Ye're bored?' he'd say to us. 'What the hell has ye bored? I don't know how anyone could feel bored once he had the price of a packet of Gold Leaf like ye have. If I had that, I'd gladly stay bored for the rest of me life.'

Which is exactly what he *was* saying on the Sunday morning they went into the village of Ballingeary to await the arrival of the buses: two day-excursion buses out from Cork city with the parents, relatives and friends of the boys and girls on the *cúrsa*. A fine bright day it was, with great fleecy clouds flowing across the sky and out towards Gougane Barra and the hills beyond. The neat white cottages on the way down to the village looked as if they had been painted onto the furze and bracken behind them which were all alive with colour – a nice warm welcome for the day trippers out from the city for the day.

On the stroke of twelve, the drone of the engines came up from the far end of the village street and a big cheer went up from all of us waiting *scoláirí* as they hove into view. Johnny stood there cheering with the rest of us – but he soon stopped as, one by one, the visitors stepped down:

fathers and mothers, sisters and brothers, uncles and aunts, all hugging and kissing, hand shaking and embracing.

'Will ya look at them for God's sake,' Johnny muttered. 'Anyone would think they hadn't eaten a bit or seen each other for years. A lot of bloody Mamma's darlings.'

Then, as the goodies were being handed out – the biscuit packets and cakes, the chocolates and sweets, bags and baskets of them – the muttering got a bit louder.

'Anyone would think they hadn't eaten a bit for weeks. God Almighty, I'd give the whole lot for a packet of fags this minute.'

Then, down the steps of the buses came some of our own relations: my big brother Ken with his new wife are there, as are the parents of all the other lads who are with me and Johnny in our *cúrsa* house – and the same caper begins with us. Off we all go with them until, at last, no one is left standing in the street but Johnny alone. Just for an instant, he feels a bit bad about that. No need for the candy-and-kisses, no need for any of that. But just to have someone, someone of his own – to talk to, to say how he was getting on, to show off the new places and the new people he has come to know: his mother especially; yes, it would have been nice to have her, if only to say 'Hallo' and 'How are ya?' But for that she would have to be all dressed up in finery like the other respectable folk who had come – and what sort of finery would her threadbare coat and broken shoes make among them?

'Johnny? Are you Johnny Farrell?'

The man calling him was standing on the bus platform, the last one to come down. He had his own boy beside him and had gone back in to collect something he had forgotten, which he had in his hand now. How did he come to know his name? Boys from the alleys and lanes were always getting into scrapes – pilfering slabs of chester cake or bags of apples were not the only offence; was this some guy coming after him for that? The man beckoned him over and handed him a parcel.

'This is for you,' he told him. 'It's from your mother. She can't come herself. When she heard I was coming, she asked me to bring it along.'

Johnny took the parcel and walked away. What was in it? What had his mother sent him? He would have slipped the string and opened it but, first, he wanted to be alone: mothers could do stupid things betimes, he didn't want anyone to be around to see him when he found out what stupid thing this was.

Just up the road, he spotted a gap in the fence where the bushes parted and the furze gave good cover inside. He slipped through, trampling the briary shoots and feeling the thorns prick at his bare knees. A blackbird flew up in panic; Johnny stood still until she was gone and the leaves settled where she had stirred them. At last, he was alone. He slipped the string on the parcel and opened it.

Inside were four Crunchies, four packets of gum-sweets, four chocolate bars, a large Toblerone and four iced cakes. Under the cakes and stained by the icing from them, there was a single sheet of ruled paper torn from one of his own school jotters:

Dear Johnny,
Just a few lines to let you know that we are all well as I hope this finds you out there with all the other nice boys and girls. Christy says the bed is cold at night without you and when will you be back. Dad will be a year dead come Sunday, say a prayer for him, he was a good Dad to us while he could. I must close now as Mr Fitzgerald, the man, is waiting. He has a little boy out there too, do you know him? I hope you do, I'd like to see you making friends with nice boys not like some of them around here. Say thanks to Mr Fitzgerald and share some of the things with his son if you like in case he doesn't get much. I

hope you like them, they're your favourites, it being
Saturday and the big shops shut they're all I can get.
Remember what I said about getting your feet wet.
And, dear Johnny, don't forget what I said about say-
ing a prayer for Dad come Sunday.
Love from Mamie, your Mam

The chocolate bars were indeed his favourites, the gum-
sweets had a chocolate covering too but with a hard centre you could get a good chew on. He took one of the
chocolate bars and slipped off the cellophane wrapper. The
rich smell of the chocolate in his nostrils and the humming
of the bees in the fuchsia bushes told him he was as free
now as they were to enjoy the good things life had sent
him. But then, slowly, he put the wrapper back on; and,
coming out through the gap in the fence onto the roadway,
he headed back to the house.

It was late that night when the buses left the village to
return to the city. When the rest of us finally got home,
Johnny was sitting up waiting; he beckoned us out and
down to the barn, where he opened his parcel and spread
his stash of goodies out before us.

'Look what I've got here,' he tells us. 'Look at all this
crap the ould wan sent me: chocolates and sweets and cakes
– for me, for Christ's sake. What d'ye say, fellas? Ye all got
cash from your folks today – tell ye what: I'll sell ye the lot
cheap, all I want is enough for one packet of twenty Gold
Leaf.' It was not hard bargaining: the coins came fast and
free, it was all over in a few minutes, a mini-auction and
the buyers well pleased. Johnny counted the scattered coins
that had been tossed before him onto the paper wrapper.

'Three pounds seven shillings. Boy oh boy, this will
keep the home fires burning for a week!'

The following morning, before any of the rest of us was
awake, he was up and dressed and off down to the village

street, the loot of the previous night rattling away in the inside pocket of his reefer jacket. The street was quiet now, all the clamour and excitement of the buses and the visitors yesterday was well gone. The little old lady in the post office was sitting primly behind the grille: a timid, bird-like creature, surrounded by her shelves of ledgers, books and records, with the boxes, bottles and jars of the other side of her trade lined up on the shelves opposite them. She would have been expecting customers like this today: sooner or later, whatever cash the *scoláirí* got from their friends and relations always ended up with her.

'Yes, boy,' she pipes up pertly, looking out over her rimless glasses, 'what do you want?' Johnny reaches in his pocket to take out the three pound notes.

'Can I have a money order for that?'

'A . . . what?'

'A money order. Three pounds.' Creakily, she lifts herself off the office stool and looks sharply at him. Thin, lanky, crew-cut, fox-eyed, he has all the look and shape of the city streets and lanes about him; no matter how young they are these days, such boys can be dangerous. She looks down to where his hands are, close by his sides; but there is nothing else there, no knife or other weapon, nothing but the three pound notes.

She scrawls her initials on the money order, stamps it, and hands it out to him. He pushes the notes towards her under the grille and takes the biro which is tied to it by a string. Then, where the word 'Payee' is, he writes 'Mamie Farrell'. He puts it in an envelope, addresses it and, with the last of his auction loot, buys the stamp that will bring it home.

War Cry of the Gael

Mother had this step-aunt called 'Christina'. The second 'i' in her name was high, like a 'y', so she was not 'Christina', a nice refined class of a name, but 'Christyna', a much more remote and formidable one. How she came to be called Christyna is a mystery to me, just as it's a mystery how she came to be Mother's step-aunt in the first place: the people in Mother's life were all either bachelors or old maids or, if married, they stayed married 'till death do us part'. When that happened, they rarely if ever married again, being burnt enough the first time. But it must have been out of one of those 'rarely if ever married again' lot that step-aunt Christyna came. However she came, she came with a bang.

She was a very staid, proper and respectable person, the opposite of what Mother was. Coming up from Mass in Christ the King church in Cork on Sunday mornings, the collar of her black velvet coat up about her neck and an astrakhan cap above it, she was a short, sturdy pillar of poise and respectability with, to complete the picture, a rolled black umbrella keeping time with her measured walk. Mother would see her coming up the road and her eyes would gladden at the sight.

'Here's my step-aunt coming up,' she'd announce. 'I must go out and talk to her.' The greeting was brief and formal but, on Mother's part, quite obviously warm. She clearly wanted the neighbours to see her with this paragon of womanhood, a proof that she too could be a paragon, if only love and life had treated her a bit better. But Christyna was too remote, too self-possessed to respond with equal warmth: a few words, a few nuggets of family news – then it was 'Goodbye and God Bless' and away she'd go.

Mother would hang over the gate then, looking admiringly after her, the living picture of the woman she wanted to be.

Christyna had a big house, a sober husband and no children; Mother had a small house, a husband who was sober only when he couldn't afford to be otherwise, and nothing else but children. What was worse, Christyna's house was free, a 'soldier's house' – her husband, one Arthur, having served in the Boer War and the Great War, for which he was recompensed with his medals, his free house and two full pensions. Father had been in the Boer War and the Great War too, but the medals seemed to be the only thing he got from them. Sometimes, when things were bad between them, Mother would say that was because Father was cross, bad-tempered and could never kow-tow to someone in authority; while step-aunt Chistyna's man, Arthur, was calm, collected and would doff his hat to anyone who had a stem of authority going with them. In our father's case, she was probably right; in Arthur's, she could not have been more wrong.

For the truth is that, if ever I saw one, Arthur was the dead opposite of a calm and peaceful man. Nor was his house a calm and peaceful house. I saw this on one occasion in my young life and, believe me, one occasion was enough.

Our own house could be bad betimes when Father and Mother got at it but it was nothing to the turmoil in Christyna's when her man got going. In between such times, things would seem to be quiet enough, but that was deceptive; the echoes of the last eruption had never quite died down when new ones began to rumble, a kind of volcanic amity which, though often threatened, mostly managed to stay dormant. The main reason for this was not Christyna herself, placid though she was, and certainly not her explosive mate, but the third member of that extraordinary household – one Nance, Christyna's mother, and hence Arthur's mother-in-law, though not a scintilla of the proverbial bad side of that relationship was ever seen to attach to her.

Old as the hills she was and older – she was 98 when the last illness took her; confined to a wicker chair in the corner beside the fire; nevertheless some elemental calm and peace seemed to exude from her and spread about the house, like the protecting wings of some guardian angel over the whole tormented scene. She was the one who once said to me a thing which, as a boy of ten, I had no idea what it meant. 'Child,' she said, 'never forget that the weak things of this world are destined to confound the strong.'

Christyna loved this old woman and was hugely devoted to her. By now helpless with age and infirmity, she might certainly have been in an old people's home, where she would have been looked after by a good, caring staff; but Christyna would not hear of it, refusing to have her moved, even when she was ill, taking on all the trouble of nursing and caring herself. Her patience with the old lady was monumental, a patience which was rewarded by Nance's total trust in her. They rarely spoke, communicating in nods and smiles and bits and pieces of broken words and sentences, neither much listening to the other and leaving it to each other to fill in the gaps between the silences. At times like this, out of Christyna's small puckered eyes would come the sunshine or shadow of whatever mood was upon her; it was this, coupled with her code of exterior respectability, that made our own mother look up to her. Was there anything more to it than that, I used to wonder? How come that our careworn, care-laden mother could care so much for someone who seemed so utterly different? Had there been a time in the long-distant past, when Mother was a girl and that cold and remote respectability of Christyna's flight had been, in her eyes, the scents and perfumes of a young woman in her prime? Something so fine, so strong, so captivating that it still shone through the silent, stone-faced woman in black she had now become?

Meanwhile, her husband, Arthur, the ex-soldier, despite a usually calm exterior, could be a very angry and convulsive man. He chewed tobacco like a cowboy and rolled his r's like a broken-down film cowpoke. Nevertheless, there was a good side to him: whenever I crossed his path around the city centre in Cork, he would wink down at me from his Olympian height and slip me a shilling – a token, I suspected, of some joint conspiracy between us. But a conspiracy against what? Ragamuffin waif that I was, out of a poor house and with often-warring parents, did he see in me a small conspirator against his wife's overbearing sense of middle-class morality? Not that meeting him in the street was always an unmixed blessing: for a young fellow to be seen by his mates when Arthur got into full flight was not a sight he would be allowed to forget. He would stand bolt upright in front of me, bring the shining ferruled walking stick onto his shoulder like a rifle, and shout his regimental motto at the top of his voice: 'Fogaballa is the war cry of the Gael'.

'Fogaballa' is from the Irish *Fág an Bealach*, clear the way, the motto of the Irish Guards, with which illustrious regiment in the British Army of Queen Victoria and King Edward he had seen service, and he was not letting anyone forget it.

Straight as a ramrod he still was, though then into his seventies. He would have his chin tucked in, as if holding the chin-strap of the big 'busby' which the Guards wore on State occasions; a white silk scarf slung loosely about his neck and hanging down before and behind; and the walking stick swinging and swishing as he strode on with the style and strut of a true gallant. That was our Arthur, proud custodian of a proud regiment's honour and good name.

The trouble was that all this impressive array took assembling. And, as with most such elaborate procedures, things can sometimes go wrong. This could happen at any time; but it so happened that they went wrong on this particular Sunday morning when Mother had sent me up to Christyna on an errand and Arthur was preparing to go out to Mass. Mass was one thing, the parade down town afterwards was quite another: that was what all the pressing and polishing, the shining and ironing, were about. It was in the midst of it that I had arrived at the start of what was clearly a gathering storm.

'Me shirtstuds,' I hear him shout as I go in. 'Me cufflinks and me shirtstuds, I left them there on the mantelshelf last Sunday. Where have they gone? Has some woman tidied them away?'

'Some woman' – i.e. Christyna – gets up and goes about the place, endeavouring to assist him. She does not assist him; on the contrary, her endeavours proving useless, she serves only to drive him further into a rage. Rapidly, the missing fitments take on an evil and malevolent life of their own: they intend to stay lost; and her assistance, if such it be, implies a helplessness on his part which in no way is conducive to restoring peace. As they stubbornly refuse to be found, the notion builds up in him that this is a deliberate ruse of God, man or woman – woman principally – to prevent him doing the thing he now most lives to do: turn out in public on Sunday mornings, spick and span, the perfect image of the 'sergeant major on parade', an Irish Guards sergeant major at that.

From where I am sitting – 'cowering' might be a better word – at the far side of the fire from old Nance, I sense that something serious is amiss; the silence in the rest of the house becomes more intense as he goes stumbling and shouting about, like an elephant rampant in the jungle; it is a silence that precedes the thunder clap and lightning flash.

Very well then! If God, man and woman are going to thwart him, he will bloody well thwart them. All and sundry will quickly come to know how long they can withstand the fury of an Irish Guard. I sit there, scarcely daring to touch the slice of bread and jam Christyna has laid out for me. Up and down the stairs he goes, opening and closing drawers, slamming the wardrobe doors as the tiered order of Christyna's home goes flying all over the place. I cannot help thinking that, if I were at home and Father were to carry on like that, our mother would go for him like a woman half-mad. But Christyna stands there, calm and impassive, doing nothing more than sifting through the wreckage the tornado has left lying about, restoring order to her dismembered world. In this, Arthur senses a further challenge to his Guardsman prestige, a challenge that pushes him some notches higher on the Richter scale. This has no effect on her; if anything, it has the opposite effect, making her more imperturbable still.

'Alright,' he finally comes storming back downstairs, 'if that's how it is to be, that's how it will be. Sunday or no Sunday, Mass or no Mass, hand or foot I'll not stir outside that door until those studs and cufflinks are found.'

With that, he plonks himself down on a chair at the window and pulls the glasses down on his nose. Fortunately or unfortunately, depending on your point of view, the Sunday papers are there on the windowsill before him: Christyna has been to Mass earlier and has brought them home with her.

But, pious and observant woman that she is, she did not bring them home so that her Satanic husband might sate himself on crimes, murders and naked wonders when he should be down on his knees praying for his immortal soul. This is a canon so deeply inbred that it finally gets the upper hand of her good instincts, including her monumental calm.

'Will you not,' she quietly asks, 'for the love of God and all that ever died belonging to him, put a muffler about your neck and go down to Mass before you make a holy show of us in front of all the neighbours?'

This is the last straw: that anyone should ask a man, especially an Irish Guardsman, to go out in public on Sunday wearing nothing but a rough muffler about his neck is the brazen limit of woman's cheek and ignorance. Across the fire from where I am sitting, I hear an ominous gurgling from deep down in his chest. When it comes out, it is a strangulated roar.

'FOGABALLA! FOGABALLA! FOGABALLA! A war-cry it may once have been; for all I know, it may be one still. But for me now, a boy of ten, an impressionable one at that; for Christyna, a wife and a patient one; above all, for Nance – a woman who had lived her life for most of a century with a firm belief in God and the One True Church: it might as well be the name of the devil, the Evil One himself bringing curses down upon their house.

Nance has not lived her life for most of a century without learning some lessons in the course of it. Among them is one suited to a canny counter-attack upon the onslaught of the Irish Guards. There she sits in her wicker-chair, a round, dimpled ball of wool, swathed in her knitted shawls and skull-cap, a filigree of white hair braided across her ivory forehead. Old she certainly is, but those busy hands of hers have never stopped working: knitting, crocheting, embroidering. A houseful of fine artefacts testifies to the quality of her many crafts, some of them the proud possession of her daughter's choleric man – socks, scarves, jumpers, cardigans. In mute but genuine recognition of a dress talent not less exacting than his own, he is not remiss in showing them off: once, I spotted him on the Grand Parade of Cork, the cane swishing, the head thrown back, with his overcoat uncharacteristically wide open – showing off the handsome cable-stitch jumper she had just made for him. So, unlike her daughter who has broken her silence and her calm, there will be no breaking the silence and calm with her; at her age and stage of life, such a breach would be a black stain and an obscenity. She had lived long, had seen many alarms and crises far greater than this; there is no alarm or crisis grave enough now to disturb her imperturbability.

In addition to her imperturbability, she has another gift which the wisdom of years has given her: the gift of anticipation. If her devoted son-in-law has mislaid his shirt-studs and his cufflinks and is now calling the devil's curse down upon their house because of it, she cannily recalls that this is not the first time it has happened, nor is it likely to be the last. And, in a quiet moment when she had nothing better to do with her hands, she gathered up and put aside a little cache of them, nice white bone studs and ornamental cufflinks, the very thing to suit the dress and dignity of an Irish Guard.

'Arthur dear,' her reedy little voice pipes up, 'I think I know where there may be a few spares.' With that, she raises her dumpling mound from the wicker chair and goes to a porcelain jar. Arthur, still furious, but curious now as well, observes the tortoise progress as she goes. At least the fusillade of slamming doors and drawers has stopped.

'It's as well someone around here has a bit of sense,' he mutters, 'instead of always tidying things away.' But he is not quite finished; a final side swipe is needed to chastise the nerve of meddling women and assuage the wrath of a man so sorely tried.

'The cheek of anyone asking a man, an Irish Guardsman, to go out in public on Sunday with nothing about his neck but a common muffler!'

Christyna, now restored to her habitual calm, has learnt how to take such rebuffs in silence. 'FOGABALLA' may indeed be the cry of a strong and evil spirit; but, clearly, she – like me – has heard her mother tell how 'the weak things of this world are destined to confound the strong'.

The Lion Tamer

The Garretts lived on Monks' Walk up the road from us in Cork. There were five of them, all boys. Their father was dead, lost at sea in a winter storm before the last of them was born. So the job of bringing up her five strong sons fell to the mother, a stern silent woman, very self-contained. Not that she might have been that way by nature but, with five young boys to rear, it was essential that someone be a centre of calm. It would be wrong to take her calm for weakness. It certainly did not prevent her from ruling her house with a rod of iron – once she was around to rule; but she could not be around all the time. Thereby hangs this tale.

The eldest of the boys, Bert, was the one I knew best. He was a friend of my big brother Ken. Among my early memories is one of the pair of them setting off on a cycling holiday, with tents, sleeping bags, cooking, hiking and climbing equipment, all packed into two king-sized rucksacks strapped to their backs. Away they went, like camels into the desert, the two humps rising and falling as they rode off down the hill. When the holiday was over and they came back, Ken looked fresh and well and much the better for his time away; but he was nothing to Bert Garrett, who was burnt copper and whose pit-prop arms seemed to have got inches thicker in the few weeks they were away.

That was Bert, the eldest of the family; in some ways, the one who took the father's place. But, with all five of them close enough in age, no one really took the father's place. Bert was no more than a *primus inter pares*, the first among equals; for equals in strength and prowess they pretty well all were. The younger ones next to Bert were Sam, Harry and Tom, all cut out of granite, with close-cropped hair and raven eyes – and with the added advantage in their case that they were athletes and thought nothing of vaulting over the five-bar gate into the backyard – which, when their mother was not at home, was their favourite way of entering the house.

Then there was Tiny. This was a nickname which he had got when he was growing up, it being assumed by everyone that he would stop growing and the nickname would stop too; neither did – and Tiny became the only real giant any of us had ever seen in our lives. Unlike the rest of them, who were quiet, modest and self-effacing, Tiny had a flair for the fabulous, a flair which he seemed to delight in exploiting. He dressed in black – black shoes, black suit, black overcoat, with a mane of black hair above to make the impression complete. People would stop in the street to look at him, at this massive unbroken column of black strength. He would remind you of one of those giant spars standing out from an iceberg, proud, aloof, taut with frozen dignity.

The only ones who seemed to be totally unaware of his height and size were the other giants who lived with him. Unaware and at peace – as long as the peace lasted. But, as we know, 'the best-laid schemes of mice and men gang aft aglay'; and, in the best regulated households, things can 'gang aft aglay' too.

I was in their house on Monks' Walk one Friday evening when such an event happened. Ken had sent me up there with a puncture-repair kit for Bert's bike; they were off down to Crosshaven the following morning to spend a camping weekend there. I was actually on my way out the hall door when the row started – a row, so far as I could tell, which was to do with money. The way I understood it, it happened something like this.

The youngest of them, Tom, had just finished his Leaving Certificate but as yet had not managed to find himself a summer job. This was not at all unusual as summer jobs were not easily come by in those years. He had his name down for a few but so far nothing had turned up. That was fine, a young lad needed time, his turn would come, everything would be alright. But right then he wanted to go to the pictures with his mates and, his mother being down town somewhere, he asked one of his older brothers for the necessary cash. I don't remember which of them it was and I can't explain what sort of a black mood was on him that night.

All I know is that Tom seemed to have picked the wrong one. It wasn't only me who noticed it: soon, from behind their evening papers, the others around the room became aware of it too. Young Tom was being given a lecture on the need to find himself a summer job and not be a burden to the rest of them, looking for money for the pictures which they could ill afford. In a single stroke, all the others had their hands in their pockets and were handing him the necessary cash.

'There you are, kid,' Bert, the eldest, said, giving it to him, 'that'll see you right.' Then, turning to the one who had refused it, he added: 'What kind of a miserable bastard are you, talking to the young lad like that? Don't you know well that he's looking for a job? What do you expect him to do, go out and sweep the streets?'

In another household, that might have been harmless enough; in the Garretts' things caught fire quickly. Sensing that there was trouble brewing, I made for the door, but not before seeing the first blows struck. Once started, it didn't seem to matter who hit who first or who said what when, there were always old scores to settle and, with every second, plenty of new ones were coming up.

Apart from myself – and what could I do, a pigmy among giants? – there was no one about to stop them. The first the outside world knew about it was when a pane of glass from the front window went flying into the garden. This was rapidly followed by a second and a third, so rapidly that a neighbouring woman across the road – a woman with a squad of sons of her own and well used to trouble – couldn't help hearing the commotion and rushed out to see what it was. One look was enough.

'Jesus, Mary and Joseph,' she cries out, 'the Garrett boys are killing each other.'

A small cramped little creature she is, but brave enough in her way; what is more, she could never stand the sight of grown men fighting, brothers especially. She runs over from her own place and right into the middle of the melée in the Garretts' hallway, where the row is raging.

'Boys, boys, boys,' I hear her shriek, 'will ye give over for yeer dead father's soul? Ye'll kill each other.' The 'boys' may well be going to kill each other but they do not give over. The truth is that they don't even notice her; one slip, one mistake, one wrong foot at a time like that could well mean a black eye, a broken nose or a few teeth missing. Warfare between brothers is the worst kind, it is a fight to a finish. The neighbour woman runs around on the fringes of the lurching bodies, snatching and screaming at them, pulling her hair out as she tries to get them apart. Her cries and prayers fall on deaf ears.

Where is she to turn now? What else can she do? A helpless woman she is, with nothing but the strength of her own four bones. What help or power can she call upon to bring them to their senses?

Sergeant O'Neill of the local Gárda Síochána lives away up the far end of Monks' Walk. His is a big house, a respectable house, as befits a big and respectable man. It is not a terrace house like all the others: it stands at the corner, on its own, aloof, superior, detached – a bit like Sergeant O'Neill himself. Tall, gaunt and angular, he is; his jaw juts out in law-enforcing challenge and his cold grey eyes look out with disfavour upon a law-breaking world. As ill luck would have it, the minute the neighbouring woman comes banging on his door begging him to come to her aid, he is sitting at the fire reading the *Evening Echo*. His Garda tunic hangs loose and ungainly about his shoulders, his boots are unlaced; in a word, an appearance most unseemly for a man in authority, especially when seen by a neighbour, who is expected to look up to him.

Before coming to the door in answer to her urgent summons, he buttons himself up, ties his bootlaces, puts on his belt and cap. Now, he is ready to face the world with the full majesty of the law.

The Garrett boys are still at it as the neighbour woman runs ahead of him down Monks' Walk. They know Sergeant O'Neill well: when they chance to meet him on their way to and from work, they touch their caps to him with the respect their mother has taught them to have for a man of his standing. But this is not the friendly Sergeant O'Neill they meet on their way to work; he is certainly not the Sergeant O'Neill who, after all, is no more than any other neighbour about the place. This is an outsider, a paid, truncheon-bearing intruder, a busybody poking his nose into a row between brothers. As he approaches – menacingly, he himself thinks – the Garretts see him and turn on him as one man. 'Hit-one-hit-all' has been their motto ever since they were boys; whoever touches one of them has all five as his mortal foe.

So it is that, within seconds of his arrival, the strong arm of the law is in full flight, his sole defence against their concerted fury the little neighbour woman, who has followed hot on his heels to make sure that no harm will come to the innocent boys. She stands valiantly in their way now as he retreats to the safe haven of his fortress home. There, restored to his full official dignity, he resumes his place beside the fire, to command without further interruption his own domestic scene.

What is to become of the Garretts now? The strong arm of the law has failed; its agent having fled the scene, their quarrel regains its momentum. Bereft of further hope, the neighbour woman runs to the corner of Monks' Walk to see if help in any other shape or form can be found. Anything, anyone will do, so long as it or they are willing to lend a hand.

Great faith breeds great rewards. For in that instant coming up the road towards her, she sees the tall, silent, black-clad figure of the Garretts' mother.

'Boys, boys, boys,' she cries out, running back to them, 'give over for yeer dead father's soul. Yeer mother is coming up the road. It'll break her heart if she catches ye like this.'

The effect of this announcement upon the five warring gallants is instantaneous. Like a band gone mad, each of its members adding his own to the wild clang and clatter of noise, at a single stroke, they stop. Their hands drop to their sides as they move close to each other, silent, sheepish, dumb. What a sight they are to look at then; I have been out there at a safe remove, seeing it all: ties torn off, shirts in tatters, mud stains and blood stains all over their dark and troubled faces.

Then, as one man, they make for the front door. The splintered glass from the shattered windows crunches underfoot, the neighbouring woman hangs upon the gatepost, much afraid that it will be more of the same once they get in. She is still whimpering at them to 'give over before they break their poor mother's heart' as the door slams in her face and she is left there, alone in the silence.

Their 'poor mother' arrives and stands at the gate beside her. She looks about her – at the broken glass, the trampled flower-beds, the whole ugly devastated scene. She says nothing, just opens the door of her embattled home and goes in.

'Thank God, thank God,' the neighbour woman whimpers as she walks away. 'Please God, that'll be the end of it.'

It is not the end of it. Seconds later, while she is still within earshot, she sees something she can scarcely believe. It is the sight through the broken window of a black umbrella flailing wildly through the air; and, though she could not swear to it, the sound she thinks she hears is the sound of strong men crying.

On Top of the World

It was always a week of huge excitement when Bells Circus came to Cork. For weeks in advance the billposters would be up, great splashes of red and yellow and purple and green, with action pictures of Mac the Monkey, Coco the Clown, Leo the Lion and all the rest. But, taking pride of place over them all, and the act me and my pals most wanted to see, was Sir Hercules, the circus strongman, in fact, the billposters said, 'the strongest man in the world'.

We had come to know, the way people come to know things in small gossipy places like Cork was then, that he was the circus-owner's son. This put him in a class apart and marked him out, next to his father, Big Bell, as the most important person in the whole show. Everyone and everything moved to his beck and call: he rode the horses, tamed the lions, gave orders to the chimps and monkeys who sprang into action at his first word. Even Mandrake the Magician, who was supposed to have the power of life and death over people, had no power at all over him. To us, he was Tarzan, Superman, Batman and Robin, all in one. But the act of his we most wanted to see was the one where he lifted 'Talking Tom', the great circus horse, clean off the ground.

For this, he would get into a crimson cloak, with shoulder pads bigger than the ones you see nowadays in the American football game. Onto these the lifting harness would be fixed. He would come out, climb up a rope ladder onto a pedestal under the circus arch, with the platform for the horse down under him. Every step he took, every move he made, a spotlight would follow him. When he got to the top, there would be this almighty roar fit to waken the dead. Then, in a great big voice, he would command Talking Tom to enter. In he would come, trotting around the ring three times to the wild cheering of all of us before stepping onto the platform with a clatter of giant hooves. The noise of the hooves was bad, but it was nothing compared to what happened next.

No sooner had he taken up his position on the platform under Sir Hercules than he would begin to talk. Yes, talk, that is what I said and that is what I meant. We could see his big yellow teeth as his fleshy horse lips opened and his nostrils above them moved up and down to let the sound of his voice out.

'I CAN LIFT YOU BUT CAN YOU LIFT ME?

Sir Hercules would look down at him and smirk contemptuously before answering back.

'Yes, I can and I will. You watch me.'

At this, Talking Tom would come back with a challenge which, of course, was meant for us.

'VERY WELL, SIR HERCULES. LET THE BOYS AND GIRLS SEE YOU DO IT. AND, WHEN YOU DO, THERE WILL BE A VICTORY RIDE FOR THE FIRST OF THEM WHO GETS TO ME AFTERWARDS.'

Our response to this would lift the circus roof. Each and every one of us knew who it would be – him or herself. That's how you get places in the world, by being sure of yourself, shouting loudest so you get heard. When the shouting dies down, Talking Tom starts again.

'IS THERE SUCH A BOY OR GIRL HERE?' Out we come then in a wild rush, all clambering to be first into the ring. And there we would stay until Sir Hercules selected us, but for the fact that the ringmaster was already cracking his whip to drive us back out. Because, first, the lifting had to be done . . . Could he do it? How could he do it? Him, a mere man, even if he was Sir Hercules, the strongest man in the world – lifting a horse ten times his weight? Well, he could and he did; with our own eyes we had seen it. But that was last year, this year might be different. Maybe by now he wasn't that strong anymore? Besides, last year, other years, he had only barely done it, it was touch and go as he strained every nerve and muscle to make it happen. Would it be like that now? Had Talking Tom got bigger, heavier? And Sir Hercules not so big or so strong?

It was a chilling moment as the first drum roll broke over the crowd, Then, the lights dimmed, the shouts and cheers died down; for seconds, all was darkness until a single spotlight swept across the ring, picking out Sir Hercules, the belts from his harness hooked onto the platform with the horse down below. The drum roll swelled again, then died to a whisper; and, in the silence that followed, Sir Hercules began the lift.

We could see the straps tightening, locking him to the weight underneath. Then, slowly, inch by inch, blade by single blade it seemed, we could see the crushed grass under the platform stir as it lifted off the ground.

It is no good trying to describe what happened next. A fresh drum roll heralded the triumph, to be instantly drowned out by the roar of all us hero-worshippers cheering our hero strong man. We jostled and shoved each other to be first into the ring to win the victory ride.

With the excitement at a time like that, you can miss things. In any case, being small, I didn't stand much of a chance of getting through before the big bruisers who were all around me.

So instead I slipped away to the circus-ring exit where Talking Tom, freed now from his tackle, had already trotted and where the ringmaster, seeing me and seeing no one else near me, lifted me onto his back. By the time Sir Hercules had climbed down from his pedestal and come over, I was already up there, firmly installed. He jumps up beside me and, with a short sharp swing, has me up on his shoulders and away we go, the three of us – me, him and Talking Tom – on the victory ride.

'That's the place for you, young man,' Sir Hercules shouts up at me above the cheering crowds, 'on top of the world.'

And that is not all; for the very next thing is that Talking Tom begins to sing. Yes, sing – I'm up there above him, I can see and hear him, his husky horse's voice comes right up at me:

> 'Horsey, horsey, don't you stop,
> Just let your feet go clippety clop,
> Let your tail go swish and your wheels go round.
> Giddyup, we're homeward bound.
> We ain't in a hurry, we ain't in a flurry,
> Don't go kicking up your tail,
> We ain't in a hurry, we ain't in a flurry,
> Around we go again.
> So, horsey, horsey, don't you stop,
> Just let your feet go clippety clop,
> Let your tail go swish and your wheels go round,
> Giddy-up, we're homeward bound.'

I was all of seven years old when these momentous events took place. Family circuses like Bells have long since ceased to exist; what with power rigs, pressure hoists and God knows what other tricks of the trade in these smarter times, they hadn't a chance against the big combines. That, however, is not the point of my story, rather this: that native wit of mine which, even at seven, put me 'on top of the world' has stood to me in other ways since. At the risk of seeming trite by describing the whole of life in terms of a family circus, I never quite forgot the lesson I learned that day about what success can do for you, as I was perched up there on Sir Hercules' shoulders above the cheering crowds; nor the more important lesson about how you can make things happen by keeping your head when everyone else is losing theirs, so as to slip in unnoticed and take your chance when the chance comes. That is what gets you places in life, it's what puts you 'on top of the world'.

And, if this piece of gratuitous self-assessment seems to you a bit excessive in what is after all no more than a childhood reminiscence, let me explain: for it so happens that I met Sir Hercules again the other day, the first time I laid eyes on him since I saw and hero-worshipped him in Bells Circus all those years ago.

I had bought a suite of antique furniture for a newly-decorated room at home and had stayed out of work that morning to see it safely installed. In the removals van, when it came, was the driver, a great big hulking fellow who, at first, looked as if he was going to have to handle the whole delicate consignment on his own. But then, out of the cab beside him comes his mate – a gnarled and knotty old chap, hopping about like a gorilla; so much so that I wondered at the removals company having someone of his age on what was, to say the least, a fairly hefty job.

I could not have been more wrong. If there is such a thing, he turned out to be a born furniture remover, a real expert hand, as he swung the finely-moulded chairs and tables out of the van and into the house, as if they were feather light. Nor was it his strength alone that caught my attention, it was his skill as well: a master's touch, as he steered and turned his lumbering mate in and out through doors, up and around difficult corners, sometimes with no more than a hairsbreadth between them and the freshly-painted walls. All this I saw and, of course – my costly antiques being at stake – approved; and, as soon as the job was done, I would have thanked him and tipped him, and then promptly forgotten. But, suddenly, I hear this sound coming back to me as he clears the last of the pieces around the corniced stairwell:

> Horsey, horsey, don't you stop,
> Just let your feet go clippety-clop,
> Let your tail go swish and your wheels go round,
> Giddy-up, we're homeward bound.

Was I wrong? Could it be a coincidence? Sir Hercules long ago would not have been the only one to know the song. I wait until he comes back downstairs and then take a chance.

'The last time I heard that,' I say, 'was from a talking horse in a circus in Cork I used to go to as a boy.' His creased and wrinkled face lights up in recognition as his small puckered eyes look straight at me.

'You must have been one of the lads who rushed into the ring then? Maybe one of the bright ones who got the victory ride?'

As he is saying this, he is looking admiringly about him – let me not mince words here – at my fine, well-appointed home.

'My, but you've come a long way,' he says. 'You're right up there on top of the world, just as I used to tell those young lads long ago.'

What am I to think now? Here is this crusty and wrinkled old chap, come back into my life after many years – and he turns out to have, not alone the strength of his youth, but a memory of the very words he used then. I don't mind saying that I am beginning to have more than a mite of respect for him. . . With that, he laughs, as if he were reading my mind.

'Oh, never mind, that's just a little thing I used to say to make the kids feel good. And they loved it. God help them, they thought the horse really talked. And that I really lifted him.'

'Well, didn't you?'

He stands there, smiling at his mate, a kind of tacit – and not very flattering – collusion between them.

'How could I?' he chuckles. 'Sure, the bloody horse was ten times my weight, try lifting that yourself some time and see how you get on. It was all done by springs coiled inside the harness. When I pulled, the springs tightened and lifted the whole platform, just like a winch. It was the springs did the lifting, not me.'

He guffaws loudly as he tells me this and I laugh with him; but I am not laughing, I am right back to my childhood in a windswept tent in a circus field near Douglas in Cork, with all my pals around me. I am all of seven, the youngest of them – and the magic wand that touched our world to wonder then is smashed in pieces. I say nothing but fumble in my pocket for a tip and send him packing.

As he climbs back into the cab beside the driver, I hear him cackling away merrily; no doubt enjoying the idea of gullible folk who think they own the world – and yet believe that a man can lift a horse! Well, he knew who owned the world: men who can lift horses, furniture or anything else you care to mention – and let gullible folk like me pay them to do it. Sir Hercules, young or old, would always be 'on top of the world'. Which may be fair enough – provided you see the world upside down.

A Man's Best Friend

With money and how to come by it being the burning issue in all our lives in those days, you can imagine that having enough to be able to afford the price of a pedigree dog would not have been the most pressing of our needs. Other things were more urgent, like bread and butter or getting Father's one good suit out of the pawn on Saturday, so he could dress up and go down town on Sunday morning. In that sort of situation, spending money on a dog would have been an absolute outrage.

But a pedigree dog was what I most wanted, in fact it was the big dream in my life. From way back I had had this dream, ever since I took a fancy to dogs in the first place; not classy, pedigree ones, but any old mongrel at all, which I would get as a pup and trail behind me, up and down the length of the Dyke Walk beside the River Lee; a shaggy boy with a shaggy dog, but always with the secret ambition that, one day, it wouldn't be a mongrel like that I would have in tow, but my very own prize greyhound.

She would be a beauty, this dog would; a shining, dazzling streak of lightning on the track, as far ahead of all other challengers as the mongrels I then had were often the whole length of the Dyke Walk behind me. Sometimes, in the cool of the evening, when the wood pigeons were cooing in the beech trees and the flies were out over the river, I would stand there and dream about her. A slim, sinewy creature she would be, with a sharp muzzle and bright eyes, wide in the chest for wind, strong at the rear for drive, the dog of all dogs, one that would leave other prize-winners on the track standing. The more I thought about it, the wilder the dream became: in time, there might even be a monument to her! Up on a pedestal on Blackpool Bridge she'd be, her muzzle cutting the wind blowing down from Dublin Hill, with me up there beside her holding her by the lead, like that famous 'Master McGrath' who, in his day, had beaten all comers, including that great 'Rose of England' I used to hear Father and his cronies singing about when they came back up from Curry's pub near the North Gate Bridge on Saturday nights:

> The hare he came round, 'twas a beautiful view,
> And swift as the wind through the green field he flew,
> Rose gave the first turn all accordin' to law,
> But the second was given by Master McGrath.
> Great ladies and gentlemen gathered around,
> But the 'Master's' own master gave out a brave sound:
> 'For yous nobles of England I don't care a straw,
> Here's a hundred to one on my Master McGrath.'

But, with the few pence I got from Father when he came up from Curry's on those weekend nights, how could I ever rise to the price of a dog like that? Even if I were to save every penny I got, I would never come within an ass's roar of it. So, better forget about it, put it out of my head, carry on with the mongrels I had, make the best of them. For what is the use of moidering yourself with crazy dreams that can never come to anything? I am all of twelve years old by now. If it didn't come to something soon, it never would – unless the wheel of fortune turned and something happened.

Something did. It was a job, a tricky job, one for a young fellow who knew dogs – which, to be fair to me, I did. The mechanical hare ran on a rail on the Mardyke dog track and, as it came to the finishing stretch, someone was needed to stand by at the stop lever, run onto the track and, with the greyhounds in full cry coming up at him, clap a steel box over it before they tore it in pieces. It was not a job for a nervous boy; it probably wasn't a job for a boy at all; but money was short and the hours were long, no man could be got to do it – so the track owner was more than pleased when I turned up to offer my services.

'You'll have to be quick, boy,' he warns me. 'That hare thing costs big bucks, we can't afford to have it torn in pieces every night. You won't take fright now when you see the dogs coming at you?' 'No,' I assure him, 'I will not take fright.' I tell him about my own lot and how I can handle them when they get into fights with other dogs: a touch here, a jab there, a short sharp kick when they don't seem to be responding. Take fright before dogs? That's about the very last thing I will do.

'Very well then,' he says. 'Be here at seven on Monday night. We'll do a trial run first.'

The trial run goes fine: no fright, no nerves, no nothing; I just pull the stop lever when the time comes and run out onto the track with the box and clap it over the hare as it speeds to the finishing post. It is all done, and done with ease, in a few seconds. Even the greyhounds that were used in the trial run gather around me, nosing and shoving each other aside to get close in for a pat on the head. In a word, in five minutes flat, I am a young man gainfully employed.

So every race night from then on, the wooden hut beside the finishing post on the dog track will be my abode.

'The bloody kid is bred to it,' I overhear the owner say to a trackhand one of those nights. 'You'd swear the ould dogs loved him, the way they run up around him, licking him all over, just as he's robbed them of their prey.' Maybe they did. What is more to the point, I loved the five-pound note which was clapped into my fist every night after the last race. With that, week after week, my big dream was at long last going to come true.

I chose my dog well: a fifteen-month-old brindled bitch of a sire who had swept the boards in Munster and a dam who, in her day, had run all comers into the ground. A beauty she was to be sure, and no doubt about it; just as I had imagined her in those dreamy days and nights along the Dyke Walk long ago: deep in the chest for wind, not a pick too much flesh to slow her down, 26 inches from the ground, though not much more than a pup, and four sinewy legs rippling with go. Oh, a champion to be sure, she had all the marks and signs of it.

What would I call her? It would have to be something striking, something personal, yet something too that would match the great things she was going to do. Walking her down along the path beside the river at the Dyke Walk, watching the pigeons in the beech trees and the flies hanging low over the water, I could hardly help thinking of all the times I had gone by there, dreaming of having a dog like this. Now I had her. What else would I call her but the name of the place where I had those dreams – Dyke Walk?

I say it out loud and, at the sound, she cocks her ears and looks up at me.

'Oh, but you're the smart one, my lady,' I tell her, patting her on the head. 'But don't forget that no dog is smart until she's smart on the dog track.'

Then the training begins. Each night, I have her out on the flat fields beyond Blackpool, where my pals, Pa Connors and Danny Joe Buckley, hold her on the lead, while I run away off into the distance; once far enough from her I clap my hands, Pa and Danny Joe slip the lead, and away she comes, hind and fore legs going in mighty bounds, the paw pods barely touching the ground. There can be no shadow of doubt about it: she is a champion alright. Wait, just wait, until I got her onto the track.

But already, out there on the flat fields beyond Blackpool, with nothing but the long grass and the bullrushes to prevent me seeing it, there I was making my big mistake. For, between there and the dog track there would be one big difference. And, like many another dreamer before me and since, it would be too late before I saw it.

It was her first outing and, as the only unknown dog in a field of seven, she was the rank outsider. It was a late October night, with a touch of frost in the air and no moon, a grand night for racing and well suited to her. As I led her down the track side, I could feel the power of her pull on the lead, filling me with a thrill of excitement I had never felt before. The place was dark above the haloes of white light along the course; in the darkness beyond the lights, I could see the hundreds of faces in the crowd on the stand, all people who knew nothing, and cared less, about me and my pipe-dreams. What matter, people with dreams get used to living alone with them; and I was happy to live alone with mine. I looked down at her and, as I did, I declare to God, her left eye opened and shut in what was clearly a wink.

'That's my girl,' I whisper as I hand her over. 'Go out there and win.' Then, off I go to my wooden hut with its box and its stop-lever on the far side.

She is drawn on the outside, the worst possible trap. But it makes no difference; she is out of it like a streak and away ahead of the field in seconds. First, the short town stretch, then the long straight beside the river, then the bends. Away ahead she is all the time, and stays that way. I can hear the hush coming down on the crowd, not the usual hush before the last lap; this is something else, for nobody can make out who she is. 'Dyke Walk' the card says; no one has ever heard the name before. The cheering that always starts up at the last lap does not start up at all. There is nothing but the same hushed silence as the plumes of breath from the hundreds of people gathered there rise up into the cold night air.

In my hut at the finishing-post, I watch her – and am I proud? This is my dog, my champion, the one I named 'Dyke Walk' after all the nights I spent up and down there, dreaming of a moment like this, hoping, doubting, wondering if it would ever come true. Now it has. She is still away ahead at the second last bend, with only the long straight stretch to go.

Then suddenly, mysteriously, she slows. The other dogs come up behind her, closing the gap between them: the favourite, Handy Jerome, Power of Passion, Bandon Lass, Inniscarra Dame, Rodney's Choice – stragglers all compared to her, yet here they are rapidly gaining ground. I stand there stupefied. What has come over her? Has she been doped? How could she be doped when I never left her out of my sight? In any case, why would anyone want to dope her, nobody knew she was that good. Maybe it was the track lights then, something she had not seen until that night? Were they blinding her? She courses along, a few lengths ahead of the others, but they are still gaining ground. Is this Dyke Walk at all? Has there been some mistake? Did they get her mixed up in the traps and field some other dog? Because this is surely not the dog I saw with my own eyes cover half a mile of ground in half a minute.

Angry, ugly fears rise up inside me. Something bad has happened, something I do not know about, some trick or treat in this coursing game which the big guys are in on but I am not. Whatever it is, it brings all my fine dreams down in a heap around me. With only the straight stretch to go, she cannot recover now. So, I pull the stop lever and, with my box aloft, I run out onto the track.

With that, it happens. The minute she sees me, she springs to life and, with mighty strides, comes bounding on, burning up the gap between us, leaving the others behind as if they were running in slow motion.

And then, then at last, I see it – the mistake I made out in the flat fields beyond Blackpool: I was her hare, she would run to me, but to nothing or no one else. I lift the box and slam it home on the hare as she comes up on me, the others behind in hot pursuit.

They are not the only ones in pursuit; the commotion is everywhere. Shouts and curses and angry noises are coming from the crowd on all sides, all directed at me. Good money has been lost, the losers want to know why.

'The little bastard pulled the lever too soon.'

'He ran onto the track before the race was over.'

'Get him, gut him, the little get.'

'Don't let him get away.'

I look frantically towards the hawthorn fence standing between me and the river. A cold mist hangs over it, white frost is beginning to show on the grass on the far bank. Frost or no frost, I have to go on. It is either that or, at the very least, a bad hammering.

I get to the fence, scramble through and, without further thought, jump in. Seconds later, I am across the river and clawing my way up the bank on the far side.

But still I am not safe, the angry crowd are following, hell-bent on getting me. No sooner have I gained a foothold on the bank than I hear another splash. The freezing water clings to my clothes, my arms and legs are heavy with the weight of it. But, heavy or light, I have to go on. I stumble along the muddy bank but, as I do, something flashes past me, then turns and comes back. And there she is, Dyke Walk, her wet muzzle nuzzling at me, her frozen paws clawing me all over.

Lords of the Beast

It all happened when Danny Joe and I were left in charge of Foxy Jim's farmhouse. How we came to be left in charge in the first place is a good question. It had to do with the Ballinrea Races, a point-to-point held on the flat plateau near Carr's Hill on the Cork to Crosshaven road, the big event in our lives every St Patrick's Day. Danny Joe and I were always there; it was such a regular thing for us that, years later, when we were all grown up and gone away from home, the memory of the Ballinrea Races came back to me one day and, on the spur of the moment, I penned this bit of doggerel to keep time with the sound of the galloping horses:

> Danny Joe had the shillings and I had the pence
> But we made the one bank of our money,
> Which bought cakes and Tanora gulped down in advance –
> for the first race we'd catch if we hurried.
> But, it wasn't the shillings, it wasn't the pence,
> Nor the cakes and Tanora gulped down in advance
> But the way that they all turned life to a dance
> On the day of the Ballinrea Races.

Now petal-cheeked Danny is a navvy in Wales
And comes home once a year to his mother;
But it just doesn't do if he's lonely to fail
To return at the end of his tether.
For Danny, like me, is a cog in a wheel
That must be kept going despite what we feel;
And everything therefore must go under heel –
Like the trampled-down, trodden-down grass of the field
On the day of the Ballinrea Races.

That was all away off in the dim and distant future, never thought of or dreamed about in those early days. Right then, we were just two young fellas left in charge of the house and farm, Foxy Jim and his whole family – all his farmhands too – having gone off to the races, where he had a horse running that day. How come, you may ask, that we pair could be persuaded to stay away so as to keep an eye on the place? Well, I was the milk helper with Foxy Jim's daily milk round in Cork city and Danny Joe helped with the milkround of the adjoining farm of Toddy Ryan. We were strong little chaps, both of us, and well-known to them; we knew the place and could be trusted to see that nothing went wrong. Besides, a pound between us was big money, which was what Foxy Jim handed me as he clapped the hat on his head before going off.

'There's nothing for ye to do only keep an eye on things,' he told us. 'A truck will be calling for the cow over in the small byre. Just show the man where she is and draw the bolt after she's gone.'

A simple task, you could say, and not something to cause any trouble. But, even at that age, I had come to realise that simple tasks that don't cause trouble can sometimes cause the worst trouble of all.

As you will know by now, Danny Joe and me are townies, like all our people before us – Cork city folk from the warren of lanes and alleys off Shandon Street and Blarney

Street, with the North Gate Bridge down below, keeping us safe from the savages on the south side; and the bells of Shandon warning us every quarter hour against the worst savages from beyond Blackpool on the north. Sure, we know what farm animals look like; we have often seen droves of them being brought in to Marsh's Yard beside the river or the Farmers' Union slaughterhouse across the road at Anglesea Street. But that's about it. Apart from Foxy Jim's and Toddy Ryan's horses which we know from the milk rounds, we never have anything to do with their farm animals at all. Cows, heifers, bullocks, bulls, they are all one to us – unlike the horses, they are heavy, sullen creatures with cloven hooves and horns, to be kept at a safe distance from our townie lives. But now, here we are being left alone in charge of a farm and farmhouse, where a truck will shortly call to collect a cow from a cow byre; and we are to help by showing the man where she is.

Danny Joe looks out the window and sees the truck pull in. It has a driver and his mate, a young fellow not much older than Danny Joe himself, a fine strong young bloke and quite tall for his age. Seeing the jaunty strut of this chap, he decides to take the initiative and show him who is in control around here. He takes Foxy Jim's blackthorn from the hall stand and heads for the cow byre, with me and the two others bringing up the rear behind him. Looking at him striding ahead of us, you might, if you had a mind, begin to think of him as a young toreador-in-training, heading for his first bullfight. But he is no toreador – in training or any other way; he is a townie chap like myself, with a blackthorn stick, about to approach a cow, hoping that the sight of the stick will tell that gentle creature who is the boss.

He draws the bolt on the cowbyre and we stand there waiting, all four of us, driver, mate, Danny Joe and me. Townies we may both be but, from our time with Foxy Jim and Toddy Ryan, we know that farm animals can be biddable enough – once the bidding is made loud and clear.

Just a few short sharp words will do and Danny Joe says them; they are the same words that I hear Johnny the cowherd using when he wants to shift animals about: 'Wo, wo, come up there, come up'. Sounds fine, it does, has the right ring of command to it; but the ring of command rings hollow in Miss Dora's ears. From inside the rank and sultry twilight where she is having a bit of a snooze for herself, comes a heavy-chested 'MOO' as she shakes her big brown head at us. 'Aw, g'way, it's far too hot' is what the 'MOO' is saying. She shifts her weary weight from one rump to the other resolutely refusing to present to us anything but the sight of her unlovely backside.

What is be to done now? I have the feeling that, motherly creature that this is, she will sense the pickle we are in and go where she is meant to go without further trouble. She does not. Motherly creature she may be but, as Danny Joe and I well know, mothers can be dragons when they want to. She stands there, solid and stout, totally oblivious of us and the masterly world we represent. Meanwhile, the driver and his young mate standing in the background behind us begin to wonder what the delay is about; they begin to see, as we have begun to see, that the delay is about nothing but ourselves. Danny Joe stands there, stock still, the blackthorn hanging idly in his hand; I have the clear impression that I, standing beside him, have caught the infection from him; after all, he is bigger and stronger than I am and what's more, he has the stick. If he can't get Miss Dora to 'Wo, wo, come up', how can puny me? Even the good creature herself seems to be aware of it, to have picked up the message that this is not going to be any ordinary old cow-collecting job at all.

'Give her a prod of the stick, for Chrissake!' comes the rough order from behind us.

Neither of us, Danny Joe nor I, likes to be given orders; rough or smooth, it's all the same. We do not like it for two reasons: first, we do not like it in itself, especially when it comes from a culchie yokel from beyond the bounds of our noble town; second, because anyone with a blackthorn stick driving a cow having to be told what to do with it seems to us a pretty bad sign. It is even worse: for what will 'a prod of the stick' do? Supposing he prods and the prod hurts, then there will be no doubt in Miss Dora's mind who did the prodding. With the pair of us penned in there in the narrow byre, with the four walls about us and nothing but a puny blackthorn to hold her off, she has us at her mercy. Where can we run to, where can we turn for help and succour then?

There is a further problem. Believe it or not, the idea of cruelty to animals comes hard to the true townie mind. This may be because we are fond of cats, dogs, birds and other domestic pets, a fondness which transfers to the whole animal creation. The only thing we seem to be good at hurting is our own kind.

So, as Danny Joe hesitates with the stick poised to 'give her a prod' of it, I see the two country yokels looking curiously at him: is the look one of pity, or is it something worse – mockery or scorn? There is a deadly silence, broken only by the sound of Miss Dora munching and chewing while breathing heavily into the rafters. Somewhere in the distance, a cock crows. Another bad omen – the whole animal world rallied into action against the townie intruders?

She stops munching and swings her big sullen head towards us. Then comes a 'MOO' which is not an ordinary 'MOO', it is a threat.

'Prod me with that stick, you townie get,' it says, 'and I'll have you out of here before you can bless yourself!' The 'MOO' is so loud, so menacing that it shocks Danny Joe into action. The blackthorn shoots up – in terror or in self-defence, I know not which. Dora sees it and sidesteps. The next thing, she has the head down and is coming at us.

'Shut the gate, ya gobshite,' the truck driver shouts. 'Keep her in till we get the ramp down.'

A fellow who can think straight at a time like this is a brave fellow. Aside from that, he is a fellow who knows animals. All I know is that, if I do as I am told and shut the gate, Danny Joe and me are in there inside it, so we are all alone with her; locked in, penned in, trapped in, call it what you like, it's all the same – we are on our own with a wild animal coming at us. Whatever other dreams and ambitions we may have, we have none at all to be remembered as the first and last of the cow-fighting toreadors.

Dora makes for the now-open gate but, if she does, we make for it with her. Her broad haunches sweep past us, her hooves stumble on the farmyard cobbles, then she is gone. Danny Joe and I are left standing there, alone at the cow-byre gate – our staff of office, the stout blackthorn, hanging limply between us.

The moments that follow as we go after her are a nightmare of acrobatic dives and plunges, of the other pair shouting and bawling at us, of nettles, briars and brambles scraping and stabbing at us, of a murderous nest of barbed wire planted with devilish cunning in our path, and another which swims out like a shark hook to catch us in full flight. But, above all, it is a memory of that spry and sprightly lady leading us a merry dance through pastures green which, to our cost, we soon begin to realise that she knows far better than we do.

At last, we give up, we can follow her no longer. Meanwhile, in spite of the fun and games they are having at the townie boys' expense, the driver and his mate are getting impatient. The driver is a heavy, cantankerous bloke; a fellow of few words, most of which begin with F, B and E, the latter of which stands for 'eejit' – I leave it to your imagination what the other two stand for. His young mate is different, he is the kind who grows like a rash on you and the only way you can deal with him is to scratch and tear at him till he comes to pieces. All through our royal hunt he has stood aside, sneering, smirking, which drives us mad entirely, seeing that it is his job more than ours to get this cow in. Yet there he is, taking advantage of our good nature, in order to stand by himself and do nothing.

But now things have got to a point where one or other of them must take a hand. The mate comes forward, cuts a stick from the fence and stands in the gap leading up to the truck. The idea is that we will drive her ladyship towards this gap and then he will take over: she will see that the game is up and, with us driving her on and him waiting in the gap to steer her, she will go tamely up the ramp and that will be that.

That will not be that; something else will, something that restores our shattered townie confidence and tells us we may not be as big an F, B and E as his foul-mouthed driver friend has said. What we hear is not so much a shout as a squeal, like that of a trapped rabbit with the dogs about to pounce. It comes from the sneering, smirking know-all, standing in the gap.

'Run, run, one of ye. Get down here quick, for Chrissake, I'll never be able to stop her getting through this gap on me own.' I have visions of that Cuchulain we read about in the schoolbooks holding the Gap of the North against the armies of Queen Maeve of Connaught. Ho-ho then, what sort of a funky Cuchulain have we here? He has the ash plant aloft in his hand but as Dora comes at him driven on by us, she sees enemies before her and behind; but her forward gears are in motion now, so it's him she goes for first. By the time she gets there, he is gone.

And she, big though she is, prances through the gap he has deserted and heads off into the far field. By the time Danny Joe and I get to him, the sneering, smirking little get is standing there with his hands hanging – and the ash plant hanging helplessly by his side.

'It wasn't my fault,' he moans. 'Ye eejits were driving her at me too fast.'

Now, finally, it is time for a real man to take a hand. Up to this, the truck driver has stood to one side, waiting for things to happen which would let him get back into his cab and be on his way. But things were not happening; and, if they did not happen soon, he could well be there all night.

He walks quietly towards Lady Dora, where she is grazing in the lush grass, having shaken off the last of her pursuers. His walk is a confident walk, the strut of a man who knows what he is at. These three 'F, B and E's', he seems to be saying, have failed in the simple task of getting a cow into a truck; what else could you expect from milk-and-watery townies, at least two of them never spent a day on a farm in their lives. He would teach them, he would show them how.

He comes towards her, using the same 'Wo-wo-come-up' routine that Danny Joe had used. But this time, having heard it once too often, Lady Dora runs at and past him and, with a toss of her head and a stampede of hooves, heads off merrily into the open spaces beyond.

This time, she is gone for good. Away off down the drive she goes, laughing her heart out, if cows can laugh, at these lords of the beasts who can be such 'F'n B's and E's', whenever a beast takes it into her head to defy them.

Then comes our final disgrace. Half an hour later, she is back; a couple of local lads find her, up to her arse in a ditch, from which, with some difficulty, they haul her out and herd her back to us. The first thing she does when she sights the four gallants who have tried to trap her is to stop in her tracks and utter a great big 'MOOOOO'. Never in my life have I heard a sound so loaded with mockery and disdain. Then, with the walk of a queen, she steps onto the ramp and saunters up, while half a dozen of the sisterhood within move to one side to make room for their new-found champion. They even have a cheer-leader. She sounds off with the lead 'MOOOOO' then the others join in. Dora stands to attention until they have finished. Then, I swear to God, she dips her head and bows!

The truck men take one last disparaging look at Danny Joe and me as they drive away.

'Did ya ever see anything as thick in your life as an F'n townie eejit?' we hear one of them say.

'Never. Haven't a bloody clue, have they? All any animal needs is the prod of a stick, then leave it to themselves to do the rest. It's what's known as horse sense.'

'Yeh, but you couldn't expect a townie gobshite to know that.'

A Conflict of Interests

St Mary's Parish Hall stood at the junction of roads at the top of Shandon Street on the north side of Cork. It was the big venue for us youngsters in those days, with our great heroes, Buck Jones, Tim McCoy and Hopalong Cassidy, up on the white screen at fourpence a time; and with the fallout even better as we galloped home down the hill, walloping the hell out of our backsides in pursuit of Red Indians. But, for the month following Christmas each year, St Mary's doubled as a cinema and a concert hall, with nightly productions of *Cinderella*, *Puss-In-Boots* or *Snow White and the Seven Dwarfs*, all taking turns on the makeshift stage. This year, it was the turn of *Snow White*; and a very good turn it was.

When the curtain came down and lights came up on the opening night the parish priest, Father Cunnane, sat in his place of honour in the front row, applauding by all means but still a somewhat divided man. This was the same Father Cunnane who used to prod the hedgerows to root out the courting couples beyond Blackpool and Spangle Hill. The courting couples were not his concern now; rather, a different problem, though of the same moral kind.

91

From the point of view of the parish funds, he had every reason to be pleased: the hall was packed, right up to the back rows of the gallery with its rickety wooden benches, and with latecomers standing three deep behind them again. There was a large parish debt, responsibility for the clearing which was his. With a capacity house like this every night for a month, he would make a big dent in it – how else should he feel but pleased? It was a windfall that would not come his way for at least another year.

And yet, as he sat there in his place of honour, he was an unhappy man. He had seen the worm in the rosy apple and, much as he might want to, he could not bring himself to eat it now.

He wiped the mist from his gold-rimmed spectacles and waited for the last of the enthusiastic applause to die down. Then, with a word here and a word there, he made his way through the audience up to the makeshift curtain which was draped across the entrance to backstage. Beyond that was a long passageway to the dressing rooms, where he could hear loud voices, shouts and laughter, the kind that comes with the loosening of first-night nerves. He walked quickly past those rooms, not wanting to meet up with the people there. He had other, more important, business on his mind.

At the end of the passageway, he came to a door marked 'Manager Private' and knocked.

'Yes,' came the voice from within, 'who is it?'

'It's me, Father Cunnane.'

'Come in, Father, come on in, there's no need for you to knock.' There was no mistaking the cheerfulness in the man's voice. He was a small fat chap with a shock of grey hair and a face as florid as a rhubarb leaf. On the table in front of him lay the night's takings – large stacks of notes and a pile of scattered silver coins.

'Well, Father,' he pipes up delightedly, 'you will have good reason to be a happy man tonight.'

The priest looks at the piles of cash and does not disagree with him.

'Well done, John,' he says warmly, 'it looks as if we may be onto a winner with this one.'

'You can rest assured of it, Father. Wasn't it worth all the trouble and effort now? For the past month the cast, the producer, everyone involved worked their backsides off for this – if you'll pardon the expression.'

Father Cunnane pardoned the expression; but that is not to say that he liked or approved of it. There was much about St Mary's Hall – indeed, about the whole unruly parish of St Mary's – of which he did not approve; but perhaps this was not the time to say so.

'Indeed, John, I can well understand that a great deal of work and preparation went into tonight's performance. Let me be the first to congratulate you – you and all the others concerned. It is indeed a most satisfactory night for us all.'

He paused, wondering – not for the first time – how he was going to approach the delicate matter he was about to bring up now. Seeing the piles of much-needed cash on the table, he found himself thinking briefly, he hoped not irreverently, of Jesus in the Temple, lashing out at the traders and hurling their money-grubbing tables out of the holy place. But he would have to be careful: there was that parish debt to be cleared and this would go a fair distance towards clearing it.

'Again, John, I repeat that it is a most satisfactory night and my thanks to you and all concerned for the work you've put in.' He paused again, pursing his lips in that stern and prudish way many shocked young lovers had seen as he prodded them out from the honeysuckle bushes on the sultry summer nights.

'And yet, if I may, John, I would like to enter one small reservation.'

'A reservation, Father? A reservation about what? Is it about something in the show?'

The priest caught the note of concern in his voice and hastened to reassure him.

'Now, now, John, there's no need to get alarmed. It's just a small point, a personal point if you like, something in the show itself which you and your people might care to have another look at.' A chill crept about the place and the manager's cheery voice dropped a little as the smile died on his rhubarb face.

'Yes, Father? A personal point?'

'It's only a little thing, I'm sure something can easily be done about it.'

The man's fingers moved nervously among the scattered coins, as if drawing support from them against whatever rebuff was coming. But the stern pastor was not to be put off.

'First, let me repeat that nothing can take from the success of the show. It's a great credit to you all and, from the parish point of view, it's clearly going to be a great financial success. But, as you yourself will be the first to appreciate, John, a parish priest may sometimes have other considerations apart from the financial ones. Do you follow me?'

'I'm afraid I don't, Father. I'm at a bit of a loss, to tell you the truth.'

'Let me come to the point then. What I mean is that this is a parish function, an event sponsored by the parish of St Mary's. And, with respect, John, I do not think you can have a function like that with a Prince Charming dressed, should I say 'undressed', as that young lady was out there tonight. It was a young lady, I presume?'

The manager looked up from the money-laden table and caught the glint of the priest's gold-rimmed spectacles. In a strange and very unnerving sort of way, at that moment he felt undressed himself, as if all the sins and secrets of his past life had been dragged out in public before him.

'Of course it was a young lady,' he confirms. 'That is the custom, Father. Prince Charming is always played by a woman. And that is her usual costume too. It's how she appears in all the pantos.'

'That may be so, John. I don't for a moment question your superior knowledge in these matters. But, in a show sponsored by the Catholic parish of St Mary's, we should surely have higher standards. I hope we can do better than ape the customs and manners of the brassy halls and show places down in the city.'

The manager looked at the cash-laden table, then at the rotting wooden skirting-boards and the broken linoleum on the floor. At that moment, he would have given much to be the manager, or even a doorman, in any of the brassy halls and show places down in the city.

'But the parish needs the money, Father,' he meekly protested. 'And the only way we'll get it is by putting on good professional shows. Prince Charming in *Snow White* has to be a young woman, and her usual costume was what she was wearing out there tonight.'

'Well, John, as I say, you know more about these things than I do. But I have yet to see someone claiming to be a prince coming out in public in what might well be mistaken – if you will pardon the expression – for a common striptease.'

The manager sat there, silent and abashed; though, if the whole truth were to be told, he would have to confess how much he personally looked forward to the striptease, not just on the opening night, but on all the other nights to come.

'Isn't that just what I'm telling you, Father?' he bravely persists. 'That is the standard costume and the audience are well familiar with it.

'Standard, John? Whose standard? I hope not the standard of the Catholic parish of St Mary's. I don't think we can honestly stand over standards like that. What about all those young men and boys out there tonight looking at her? Imagine the effect it is having on them when an attractive young woman comes out in front of them half-naked?' The manager did not have to imagine it: he knew it full well in his own blood and bones. But then was it only in the parish hall of St Mary's that they would see such sights?

'With respect, Father Cunnane,' he reminds his concerned pastor, 'can't they see the same or worse any night of the week in the cinema or on television? Indeed, Father, our Prince Charming is very modest compared to some of them.'

The priest now comes over to confront him at the table and looks him straight in the eye.

'I'm surprised at a decent, God-fearing man like you saying a thing like that, John. Surely you're not comparing what happens in the pagan world of cinema and television to what goes on in my parish hall?'

'Indeed I'm not, Father. But, whether it is in the parish hall of St Mary's or in the cinema or television, the receipts count the same either way.'

A moment of silence follows this brazen thrust. In that moment, the manager knows he has made a point. Now, to press it home, he makes it even stronger.

'Of course, we could change things, Father. That's if you insist.'

'How would you propose to do that, John?'

'Well, I'm not the producer, I'd have to consult with him. But, if necessary and if he was agreeable, I suppose we could ask the costume people to run up something else in a hurry.'

'Like what, John?'

'Oh, I don't know. Maybe a silver-sequined trouser suit or a pair of bright pantaloons, something like that. It wouldn't look the same, of course, and it certainly wouldn't be as attractive. There's this too: we'd have to explain to Prince Charming, in fact to all the cast, why it was being done.'

The priest's eyes fell once more on the stacked notes and the piles of coins spread about the table.

'How do you think they would take it?'

'Well, they would have to take it, Father, since it was coming from you. After all, it's your hall, there would be no pantomime without that.'

'I don't mean the cast, John, I mean the audience. How do you think they would react?'

'Well, Father, that's hard to say until we try. But you wouldn't want to be a great critic of the theatre now to see how popular Prince Charming was out there tonight. I mean, between ourselves and that, you heard the whistles and catcalls from the crowd whenever she came on. Of course, that could be on account of her lovely singing voice.'

Father Cunnane had noticed her lovely singing voice. Somehow, he did not think the whistles and catcalls were about that.

'Quite!' he said.

'The trouble is, Father, if it didn't work, we could be left with empty houses for the rest of the run.'

He paused, leaving plenty of time for the message to sink in.

'But, as you rightly say, Father, this is the parish hall and you are the parish priest. We would have to bow to your authority in matters of that kind.'

With that, he got up and began to gather the stacks of notes and piles of coins to put them away in the overnight deposit box. The priest helped him, now more aware than ever of their sterling weight and worth.

Seconds later, he had left the office and was on his way down to the dressing rooms. There, he warmly congratulated the cast – including the still half-naked Prince Charming – on a most successful opening night; and wished them well for the rest of the pantomime's run.

Honour Thy Father

The Manns lived up the road from us in Cork. Aside from the fact that they were neighbours, part of the reason why we younger ones had a certain feeling for them was that the father, 'The Ganger' as he was known, like our own Uncle Johnny, was a one-legged man – though, unlike Johnny, who lost his leg with the Munster Fusiliers in the Dardanelles in the Great War, 'The Ganger' Mann was much younger and had never been in a war at all. How he lost the leg I will come to but, for now, what I best remember about him was the sound of his crutch pock-pocking the pavement outside our door as he made his way down to Curry's pub on Saturday nights, with the empty trouser-leg folded above the knee. There was not much talk about artificial limbs in those years or, if there was, his wife, Eliza Mann, could not afford one.

They were an odd couple, 'The Ganger' and his Eliza. Our own mother had known Eliza from long before when she was an overseer in a warehouse where Mother also worked. That was before she married Tommy Mann, who was then a casual worker on the docks. He got his nickname from the day he lashed out at a ganger there who was giving him a rough time of it, knocking him clean off the gangway and into the narrow gap between the ship and the river wall; the unfortunate man might easily have drowned but for the timely intervention of some of the other dockers, who threw him a lifebelt and hauled him out. By the time that happened, his fiery young assailant had gone, a stowaway on another ship trading between the port of London and Cork. The docks were out for a spell for him then; so, instead, he did the only other thing left for him to do: he stayed aboard ship and became an able-bodied seaman.

Eliza's friends in the warehouse, Mother included, said 'Good riddance and I hope he's not in any hurry back'; at that time, 'The Ganger' had already shown signs of the boozing and battling brawler he would later become. Now, they could warn her even more effectively.

'Look before you leap,' they would say, whenever her sailorboy came back to Cork for a brief spell of shore leave. 'Sailors make bad husbands. They're absentee land-lords, away when you need them, at home when you don't. You could live to regret it.' Eliza took no notice. Even then, she had begun to behave like the strong, silent woman she would later be; it was her affair, her life, she did not need them or anyone else to tell her how she should live it.

So it was that, after she married him and things began to go wrong, they whispered to each other that they had told her so: a sailorboy and no good, what better could she expect? Eliza knew they whispered but kept her thoughts to herself. With the years and the bitter memory of the wrong choice she had made, Mother would say, she became the dark, silent, distant woman we would later see going up and down our road.

After Terence, their first and only child was born, there was a brief, sweet unity of wills, when they promised each other to bring him up well and give him all the things they themselves had never had. For The Ganger's part, that meant a promise to give up the sea and come back to another docks job in Cork; for Eliza, it meant a regular pay packet coming in every Friday night; so she was willing to give up her job in the warehouse and stay at home to make a good life for her home-bound husband and their son. For a time, it lasted and all went well. The pay packet came in as regular as clockwork; their one-storey, two-bedroom terrace house in Lotty's Villas was fitted out with bright cretonne curtains and polished lino on the floors. The Ganger would see the flames of a good fire burning in the grate reflected on the ceiling as he came up the Rock Steps towards his doll's-house home. But, gradually, as life settled down and he got used to things, the boredom of the brawling seafarer began to emerge; a life divided between the docks of Cork and the lace-curtained order of Lotty's Villas did not seem an exciting prospect anymore.

So the drinking began and steadily went from bad to worse. In due course, predictably, it led to all the usual stresses – rent arrears, loans to catch up with the loans, moneylenders banging on the door; which in turn led to the even wilder galloping consumption of The Ganger's binges, again and again threatening to put them out on the side of the road. By the time he was forty, he was a lost cause: rarely did a night pass that he did not come rolling up the steps to Lotty's Villas, roaring drunk and shouting challenges to come out and fight him at all the menfolk around the place. Even then, Eliza did not complain. Our own mother, who knew her well, tended to keep her distance, rightly suspecting that about the very last thing she would want to hear would be sympathy from her old workmates; but they would meet occasionally when, in various hints and half-sentences, Mother could easily tell that all was not well. In her own life, she had a certain feeling for what Eliza was going through – which, in a way, was why she knew that, for the haughty and distant person she had become, words of pity and sympathy would have been completely out of place.

For, when all was said and done, was she not much the same as all the other women in Lotty's Villas? She had a husband, he had a job, her share of the weekly pay packet always turned up on Friday nights. Indeed, Mother would say, that was one exceptional thing about The Ganger: at the start at least, he would put that in his back-pocket at the beginning of a drinking-bout and, by some extraordinary feat of will, not usual with drunks, he would hold onto it until he got home. Then, the way Mother heard it, he would bang it down on the table with such force that the cups and saucers broke, before he flopped into the one good chair beside the fire.

'Didn't I tell you you could trust me?' he would drunkenly boast. 'I promised you long ago that, drunk or sober, I would never let you or the boy down.'

Eliza would pick it up, thank him and go off to bed. Soon after, the snoring would start. She would pull the pillow over her head to shut out the noise coming at her from downstairs; as she had shut all good thoughts of him out of her heart a long time before.

So, she fought her way through the hopeless years, through all the drinking, debt and poverty, just about holding her own but no more than that; until one day down on the docks at Penrose Quay where a cargo ship was unloading, The Ganger – none the better for a bad bout the night before – walked blindly into a fully-loaded swinging container and, from then on, his working days were done. They carried him off to the Mercy Hospital, where they did what they could to put together the bits of him that were broken. But that did not include his left leg, which was too shattered to be saved. When he came to in the ward after the surgery, he began to claw wildly at the place where the leg used to be.

'What have ye done with me leg, ye bastards?' he roared. 'Put it back, put it back for Jasus sake, ye can't lave me like this. I'm strong, it'll heal, I can't hobble about like this, a bloody cripple for the rest of me life.'

It was the sad end of a sad man, a violent one too. Nothing the nurses or doctors could say or do would quieten him. He began to flail about him at anything and anyone who came near. At last, two of the orderlies got him by the shoulders and held him down, while the young house doctor got in close to give him a shot of morphine. As he went down, with the patience of professionals they explained to him that they had done what they had to do: the leg was shattered so badly that, to save the rest of him, it just had to go.

Dumbly, like a stunned animal, he turned to the wall and began to cry. Never, never again would the shouting, brawling 'Ganger' Mann be seen on the streets of Cork.

And that was the beginning of the real Eliza. From then on, she was a woman on her own. Father Cunnane – for all his hedge-prodding forays into the Black Ash and beyond after the courting couples – was a good-natured man with a willing ear for anyone in trouble. When he beard about Eliza's misfortune, he called to offer his condolences – and, more to the point, to offer her a cleaning job in the parish church and schools.

'It won't be much,' he said, 'but at least it will help keep the home fires burning until young Terence grows up. He's a fine, strong young fella, God bless him. Give him a few years more and he'll be big enough to look for a job on the docks himself. And what's a few years, Mrs Mann, when you'll have eternity for your reward?'

Eliza thanked him for his kind offer which, she said, would at least keep the roof over their heads. But it was not eternity she was thinking about; nor, much less, about a job on the docks for her son. Mother said, when she told her about it, that there was a glint of fire in her eyes and a hard bitter look about her tightened mouth. She did not say so openly but, knowing her as she did, Mother could tell what she was thinking: a job on the docks might suit the common sort about her in Lotty's Villas but it would not suit her. Her son was made for better things. She would see that he got them.

Indeed, even at that early stage in young Terence's life, it looked as if it might very well be true: for – all of us local lads growing up around the place could see it – he showed all the signs of someone who knew where he was going and was already on his way. Hadn't the headmaster in St Columba's told Eliza, in Mother's own hearing, that he had a big future – 'once he sticks to the books, Mrs Mann.' Oh, but he would, his mother would see to that; would see to it that he got every chance, every encouragement, every helping hand she could afford to give.

'Mark my words,' the headmaster proffered, 'The boy is bright. If he goes on the way he's going, he'll go very far in the world.'

Words that were meant to kindle young ambition, which they certainly did. By the time he was into his mid-teens, Terence had become an ardent and successful student; nor was there any fear that the efforts his mother was making on his behalf would go astray on him – something that was very clear to those of us who lived near them and could see how things were going.

In short, here was a heady mixture of filial devotion, with ambition and hard work thrown in, to make that promise of the headmaster come true.

He went at it with the same single-minded determination his mother had shown, never for an instant stopping to think that there might be other things, other people near at hand to which he might give at least a mite of his attention:

like his crippled and broken-spirited father, whose youth and strength were gone, and who could look now only to charity and social welfare to make up for the wreck of a life he had made for his wife and only child.

As the years went by, the gap between them grew. As one became more focussed on his studies and his life, the other became more hopeless and disillusioned. Pushed out in the cold The Ganger was then, with nothing to live for and no motivation left, a pointless and deadly rigmarole, day in day out, with no silver lining to light up the gathering gloom. It was at this stage in his life that we neighbours best remembered him, pock-pocking his way down the steps past our door to Curry's at the foot of Shandon Street, where what he had for company were other washed-up and hopeless derelicts like himself, including our own Uncle Johnny, another of the 'Johnny-I-hardly-knew-ye' brigade – only, in his case, at least he had the good fortune to lose his leg in the war, for which he had a disability pension, and a good one, at twenty-six and eight pence a week. For The Ganger, there was no such luck. So, off past our door he would go, the cap down tight over his eyes and the coat collar up against the chill wind blowing up the river from the sea – and with the few bob he could scrounge from Eliza warm in his good-leg trousers pocket. Grudgingly, she would always give it to him, not out of love and certainly not because she favoured his drinking, but just to get him out of the house for as long as it would keep him away.

And no matter how late he came back, there would be the light in the window, his earnest and improver son burning the midnight oil, his nose in the books, his thoughts a million miles from the hapless, crippled, broken-down creature his father had now become.

One of those nights, dutch-couraged by the booze, The Ganger threw open the door on the silent figure of the boy hunched over the table. He flopped into the fireside chair and stretched out his good leg towards the heat.

'I hope I'm not disturbing you, boy,' he began. 'I'll just sit here a minute to get the heat into the ould bones, then I'll be off.' Terence heard him but did not answer. He could never seem to say a word to his father now without strain. It was as if a wall of ice had built up between them which nothing from either side could melt. But now, having briefly got through it, The Ganger felt he could go on. And he liked going on, it gave him a rare feeling of paternity, a feeling too that he could be wise with the wisdom of age. It was one of the few illusions he could still indulge, an illusion which the booze in no way discouraged.

'You'd want to watch the ould health, boy,' he went on. 'Early to bed and early to rise, you know the old motto. I had no one to tell me those things, you have me. Spare yourself, space it out a bit more. When you're down, there's few will pity you.' His son wanted to stop his ears and not have to listen to this. Worse still, he wanted to answer back, to shout at the top of his voice that he wanted no advice from someone who had made a mess of his own life long ago and had no one but himself to blame for it now. But he managed to check himself and say nothing.

'Maybe it's time for you to call it a day now,' the drone from the fireside continued. 'You've been at it long enough. Just call a halt, let up a bit, have a bit of a fling once in a while. Like your father did. The ould books will wait.'

Terence was now staring at the print on the page in front of him but he was not seeing it. What he was seeing was his father's face, wrinkled and cracked and savaged by the years of booze and brawling, and loosening now to the maudlin humours which the booze was bringing on. At length, he could take it no longer. He jumped up and, as he did, knocked over the chair, alerting his mother upstairs to the gathering storm.

'You had your fling alright – and look where it got you. Call it a day, is it? Yes, and let others carry the load, like you did with my mother.'

It was all out in a single burst of rage, a moment of truth loaded with frustration, anger, blame; but with love and hatred too, locked to each other now in mortal combat. Terence's fists were clenched, ready for a fight; his father, still half-sitting, half-standing, lunged at him with the crutch; but, without the crutch to support him, his one leg slipped and down he came with a crash on the floor.

From there, when he looked, he saw his son, his only child, staring at him with a strange light in his eyes, a light he had not seen before. In there were tears, tears of fury and of rage but there were tears of pity too. The rage burned like fire, but the pity drowned the fire until there was nothing left but the lost, lonely little boy who had once, long ago, been the light of heaven in this man's ruined life.

Eliza, hearing the commotion, was already out of bed and on her way downstairs. She was his wife, a woman, she had a tongue. She had seen him like this before and had dealt with him. She would deal with him again now. A one-legged man sprawled across the floor would not put up much resistance. But respectable people, such as Eliza now was, do not like a scene.

Terence got the white-collar job he was aiming at and, for that, there was much rejoicing. From then on, The Ganger was even more on his own. His thoughts on things were no longer sought, all the domestic affairs were settled without reference to him. Like some blind Lear, he hobbled about, unkempt and unwanted, left to brood all he liked on his misfortune and rejection. But it was not to last. One win, one stroke of good fortune and he would be up again, green as the grass and ready for a new fight. Despite all his troubles and his traumas, The Ganger Mann was still a fighter.

The stroke came sooner than he expected. Not many years after Terence had settled into his fine new executive job, he was assigned to work in the same office as the daughter of the company's chairman and managing director, one Gloria by name – a name suited to her ambition. While being neither too young nor too beautiful, she would become a life companion for the fine new accounts executive who had come to work with her. In due course, with the guarantee of advancement for him and of married bliss for her, this would come to pass.

'Oho, my lovely boyo,' The Ganger crowed when he heard the news. 'The fatted calf, his Mamma's darling, she never thought he had the makings of a randy bull in him. That'll be the price of her pains, another woman making off with her treasured prize.'

And off he goes, cooing and clapping, the crutch pock-pocking the pavement on the way to Curry's in grim but fearful vengeance.

But he little knew the vengeance that was in store; and even less the woman his Eliza had now become. For, although there was a sense of loss that 'her treasured prize' would no longer be hers alone to treasure, there was also the fact that this Gloria, like Terence himself, was an only child – but, unlike him, was the sole heir to a very large fortune. Further, one of her uncles was a well-known and highly-respected member of the diocesan hierarchy, and he would do the honours at the wedding. In a word, her son – and so she – at one bound would be into high society.

That was the good side; the bad was that The Ganger, would have to be there. How could they possibly keep him out of it? Yet how could they endure the shame, the disgrace, when he got going at the wedding, and with the booze he surely would, when all the horror of the brawling sailor man would come roaring out? Eliza thought of packing him off for a month to his sister in London, where he was always keen to go, never having forgotten the docks at Wapping and his able-bodied seaman days. But how could she do that when his only child was getting married? Wouldn't it look odd, wouldn't it look strange, to all those respectable folk Gloria's parents would have along? There was an even more telling point: for, in all probability, what would happen would be that The Ganger would take the money she gave him for his fare and blow it with his cronies in Curry's before ever he got to the mailboat at all.

What should she do? Time was passing, Christmas to Easter, Easter to Whitsun, still she could think of no way. Then, with the wedding fixed for the August weekend, but six short weeks away, her luck turned.

At first, she was frightened, as the poor always are, by the sight of a policeman at the door.

'Jesus, Mary and Joseph,' she moaned, 'am I never to be out of trouble? What is it, Guard, is it serious?' The Garda was a big comfortable man, well used to the panic which the sight of his uniform in Lotty's Villas could create.

'Take it easy, Mam,' he soothed, 'it's nothing at all. Curry's is near the barracks and the squad car was passing when the row broke out. Your husband got involved but it's only a few cuts and bruises, he'll be fine. The ambulance was along straight away, he's safe and sound over in the District Hospital.'

That should have been the end of it. But for Eliza, the class-conscious, upwardly-mobile lady with the white-collar son about to marry a rich woman, it was very far from the end of it. To her, the District Hospital was what it had always been: the County Home, the free medical card hospital; not to put too fine a point on it, in her own childhood, the paupers' place. She would have to get him out of there fast and down to the private wing of the South Infirmary. Whatever it cost, she and her son would pay.

'But he cannot be moved,' the ward-sister told her as politely as she could. 'I have no authority to discharge him without the doctor's say-so.'

'You have my authority, I'll sign him out.'

'But that won't do, I tell you. The man is not well enough to be moved. In fact, he's very badly shaken. And that cough of his; mind you, we can't say anything until we see the X-rays – but I don't like the sound of that at all. Besides, when the ambulance men told him they were bringing him here, he said it was just as well, he couldn't afford any better.'

'He can't,' Eliza said, unzipping her handbag and taking out the Post Office Savings Book. 'But I can.'

'That still makes no difference, Mam. The man is in no condition to be moved.'

'Please be so kind as to get me his clothes,' Eliza snapped. 'I'll sign him out, I have a taxi waiting.'

'Well, glory be to God, I never saw such cheek, such impertinence in all my life. A sick, a dying man.'

'Dying' – she heard the word but thought little about it: in all probability, it was something the bossy lady was saying in order to impress her, to dissuade her against taking him away. She certainly could not have meant it: apart from the amputated leg long ago and the times he had a hangover from his frequent binges, The Ganger – a man she knew and had lived with down through the long years – had never been a day sick in his life. She was wrong; for he was sick now. In the South Infirmary, the X-rays showed that both his lungs were gone; and the angiogram showed three of his arteries badly blocked. When they told him this and what it meant for him, he shook his head wearily and turned his face to the wall.

'What the hell does it matter?' he mumbled. 'What's death to a man who has been dead these twenty or more years?'

Shortly afterwards, he had the first of his heart attacks and Eliza and Terence were sent for. By the time they arrived, he was in intensive care, his face ashen against the white pillows and his hands twitching above the bed-clothes. While Eliza went to talk to the nurse in charge, Terence stood at the bedside looking down at him.

Suddenly, from some forgotten place within him, tears of grief and pity came up in his throat and began to choke him. This had once been the 'Dada' of his early trusting years, a man he loved, a man his mother loved once upon a time to make what would become him. What had come over them all for it to end like this? In a convulsion of fear and helplessness, he prayed to God to give him time, just a little time, just enough for him to take his father by the hand and bring out the words that were choking in his throat now but had never yet come: that he loved him, and was sorry for all the bad and bitter things that had been said and done.

But God, it seemed, was not in a mood for barter and a few hours later The Ganger died. Terence was left to reflect on the futility of prayer; his mother said nothing. In death, her husband's lip curled upwards in an angry snarl which told her how she had failed him.

They took him to the church the following night and all his cronies from Curry's pub were there – including our own Uncle Johnny, partners together in their feckless, one-legged world. One of them, Jim Sweeney, a maudlin ould cod from up the road, in the full hearing of Terence's grandiose in-laws-to-be, bawled out his eulogy for every-one to hear.

'We'd have given our hearts out for him, Eliza. The dacentest bloody man that ever walked. Never saw any of us short, if he had it himself. He was always talking about ye, so he was – how ye stuck by him through thick and thin. And young Terence there, he thought the sun, moon and stars shone out of that boy.'

Terence heard his thick, half-throttled accent and thought bitterly: up from the mire I have surely come and some of the mire still sticks. But there was another voice besides, which was saying something else, something which had come to life only now, with his father's death. Mire or no mire, it said, no matter how high and mighty I may become, I will never now be able to do the thing I most want to do, keep the one command above all others that I want to keep: Honour Thy Father.

The coffin was closed, the funeral began to move. He walked behind the hearse, holding his mother by the arm. As they passed the mourners standing to one side to let them by, he could hear some of the parting whispers:

'God help them, the poor souls, how he loved them, the pair of them.'

'She was the only woman in the world for him. He worshipped the ground she walked on.'

'Nothing was good enough for that boy of his.'

'He had their thanks and their love at least, that was his reward.'

They were whispers that would creep into the very crevices of Terence's soul. And would lodge there to live with him for the rest of his life.

One Big Happy Family

Have you ever wondered how it would feel to meet the most important man in the world? I did – until I met him on a bleak January morning when I was all of eighteen and had reached the height of my ambition – which was to have a fine, white-collar job in the civil service.

I am in Dublin, 'a stranger in paradise', and about to cross the threshold of what will be my future working life. In doing so, I come face to face with this man across a polished desk in a darkly-varnished room.

'Good morning, young man,' he greets me, smiling avuncularly. 'So you have come to work for us. Tell me now, what do you think you will be able to do?'

I look at the bald pate, a look which is part desperation and part hope: the desperation that I had not the slightest idea how to answer him; the hope that, given time, he might come up with the answer himself. Meanwhile, behind me, a clock ticks away the agonising seconds.

'I will do whatever I am asked to do,' I say, a sentiment of such stunning originality that it must surely have come from some handbook of inspiration especially kept for raw recruits in new jobs. Whether it was what I said or how I said it, it must have struck home. The Great Man sits back in his chair and beams at me even more avuncularly still.

'Good, my boy, very good. That will do. I can see that you will suit us fine.'

I am about to congratulate myself on the success, and brevity, of this first interview when he gestures me to sit on the chair in front of him and he reaches for the telephone at his right hand. At this, I feel myself momentarily dismissed from the conversation and begin to take stock of what is happening: who is this man, this stranger I did not know a moment before, who has now come to assume a central role in my life? One thing is sure: he is no longer the anonymous 'Chief of Operations' whose illegible scrawl at the bottom of a letter has summoned me here. Now, he is someone, a real person, in fact the most-important-man-in-the-world. He is the one who will henceforth determine what is to become of me in all the years of my future working life.

What miracle of fact or imagination has made him so? The miracle, if such it be, has not happened to him, it has happened to me. For the very first time, I have come into contact with something I will never again be able to shake off – a job, a boss, pay and the obligations of pay, the mute but immutable authority of employer over employed. It is not the kindly, indulgent relationship one had had with one's parents, teachers and all other such sympathetic folk who had been one's lords and masters up to that.

Nor were the signs and symbols of authority the great and powerful things one might expect, such as a harp and shamrock, a sceptre and crown; there was nothing more here than a bald pate above a polished desk, with a clock ticking on the wall – a clock which will dictate how I am to spend eight hours of my future working days.

The most-important-man-in-the-world's call is answered and his benign, ruminant face comes to life.

'Is that you, Lorigan?' he asks. 'The Chief here. Come on up, I have someone here for you to meet.' He sounds like a prison governor summoning the head warder, an impression promptly compounded by the sound of a door slamming in the distance, followed by the tramp of what might certainly be mistaken for head-warder steps.

Lorigan, when he arrives, turns out to be not a head warder but a shop model in a pinstripe suit, with horn-rimmed glasses and lips that droop like the black stripes on a zebra. Later, when I get to know him, he will sometimes tell the story of his young son who had been bitten by a dog; this is a bad thing for any child, but this boy, being his father's son and hence a child of spirit, does not come whining home, as another might do. He takes direct and effective action himself by biting the dog back. Lorigan tells this story with lip-smacking delight: it has that touch of stern action which much appeals to his frigid mind. More to the point, it is a headline on the nature of discipline and personal responsibility; qualities, I quickly learn, which he finds much lacking in his slack and negligent staff.

'Good morning, Chief,' he says briskly, stepping in. 'You called me?'

Alert, respectful, diffident – he is manifestly the good public servant his Chief wants him to be; and frequently, if discreetly, commends him for being. Looking at him there before his lord and master on my very first day at work I know in my heart that, if I live to be a hundred, I will never live to be a man like that.

'It's about that head of staff you requisitioned,' the Chief says. 'What do you say to this young man?' Lorigan lifts his horn-rimmed spectacles to get a clearer look. He seems to take a long time making up his mind what he thinks of me. As for me, I am vaguely conscious of a primal inadequacy in not being able to sprout a pair of horns to suit my new 'head-of-cattle' status. He eyes me all over, his grave dyspeptic features a silent reprimand to my youth and ignorance. I begin to have a distinct feeling that the easy-going, indulgent world of the first eighteen years of my life is rapidly coming to an end.

'Take him away with you,' the Chief tells him. 'And make sure he has plenty of work to do. As you and I know, Lorigan, the devil makes work for idle hands. Especially idle young hands. And, as we also know, he will not stay young forever.'

Lorigan, conscious perhaps of his own ageing profile, bites on the stem of his pipe and dutifully smiles. He is not a man for jokes, except when he himself makes them. But, with his Chief, he has the duty of official respect. When it comes to duty, there are few personal prejudices Mr Lorigan is not willing to suppress.

So, the 'head of staff' is formally handed over to his drover, the second most-important-man-in-the-world, who promptly leads him off to meet the other 'heads-of-staff' with whom he is to work. Before we take leave of the Chief, however, we are treated to a further brief homily on the virtues of teamwork and pulling one's weight.

'We are all one big happy family here,' we are told. 'And I intend to keep it that way. We have no quarrels, no differences or complaints. If anything goes wrong, you come straight to me, my door is always open. Am I right, Lorigan?'

'Indeed it is,' his compliant aide confirms. 'Always open, just as you say.'

Then, suddenly, as if a floodgate had opened, a whole torrent of new words comes at me from the Great Man's desk: signing in and out on the attendance book; insubordination, suspension, dismissal, labour disputes – all words incomprehensible to this eighteen-year-old. As rapidly as they started, they stop. For, I am told, I am not to worry about any of them, just remember the one thing of consequence he has said: that, if anything goes wrong, I am to come straight to him, his door is always open.

'You will remember that, young man?'

I duly promise that I will; as I will also remember that, from that good day to the day I leave, it will never open for me again.

The room I am put to work in is a high-ceilinged cavern, with the walls painted pale green, a colour which seems to have seeped into the faces of the people who work there. Momentarily, I am reminded of Pater Damien, the saintly priest in the leper colony of Molokai: 'Abandon hope, all ye who enter here.' Mr Lorigan – no Pater Damien – introduces me to my fellow inmates; I shake hands and promptly forget their names. They do not seem to be the names of real people, more like labels stamped on them and the desks they occupy. How long will it be until I become like them?

There are piles of papers tiered high about the place and large presses and cabinets bulging with them. They have figures and signs and symbols on them, marks in red and black, yellow and green. Whose marks? And what do they mean? Will I in due course come to add to them? And, in due course, be commemorated, if not cremated, with the same fading and anonymous print?

There is a woman working at a keyboard, its keys magnetised to her slim fingers. She does not look up when I am brought over to be introduced to her, just keeps her eyes fixed on the keyboard and puts out one hand, a pale thin hand, like the claw of a bird. This is her territory, her natural habitat, her ledge upon the rock of life to have and to hold for all eternity. There are other birds of a feather all about her, male and female. Am I to become one of them now too? They are all equally absorbed, all fixed and riveted upon their given task, with no time at all for breaking the new boy in.

Finally, I am introduced to the third-most-important-man-in-the world, a tiny Rumpelstiltskin of a man, with sapphire eyes and fidgety fingers, who sits at the top desk and smiles down helplessly at me, as if to say: 'I am in this too and I know how you feel, but there is nothing I can do to help you.'

I sit at the desk to which he and Lorigan direct me and, with an application that would surely edify the Chief, set about my first day's work.

The work is the singularly inspiring one of writing receipts: receipts for cash, cheques, money orders. It is the beginning of a brain-washing that will result in thousands, maybe millions, of those faded forms stuffed away in a cobwebbed cabinet, like the cobwebbed cabinets now bulging all around me. The others have been doing this for years; Lorigan, that second-most-important-man-in-the-world, has been doing it since *he* was eighteen. Even now, as his Chief has reminded him, edging towards his retirement, he is still there long after all the rest of us have left at night, building up new records, upping the average of what is expected of each of us in our daily returns of completed work.

I do not know then, but will later know, a poem by Stephen Spender, 'The Prisoners', which tells the story of such a place:

> Far far the least of all, in want,
> Are these,
> The prisoners
> Turned massive in their vaults and dark with dark.
>
> They raise no hands, which rest upon their knees,
> But lean their solid eyes against the night,
> Dimly they feel
> Only the furniture they use in cells.
>
> Their time is almost Death. The silted flow
> Of years on years
> Is marked by dawns
> As faint as cracks on mudflats of despair . . .

When have their lives been free from walls and dark
And airs that choke?
And where less prisoner to let my anger
Like a sun strike?

If I could follow them from room to womb
To plant some hope through the black silk of the big-
bellied gown
There would I win.

No, no, no,
It is too late for anger.
Nothing prevails
But pity for the grief they cannot feel.

I do not need Stephen Spender to tell me that this will
not be a life for me. I am eighteen and do not know much;
but I know one thing: out of there I am getting, and getting fast. And, come what may after I leave, I will never go
on to become a prisoner like that.

It is a resolution that sticks. A few years later, I am gone;
the receipts, records and routines of that crazy place gone
with me. But, strange as it may seem, I do not go without
regrets.

This was mostly to do with those women, that dry and
cackling coven of witches, permanently clouded in a fog of
cigarette smoke. Gradually they at first, then more markedly, came to represent for me an extraordinary gentleness of
spirit, full of understanding for me and my teenage tem-
pers. It had been a long time since any of them had been
eighteen, longer still since they believed that there might be
the possibility of any other sort of life for them. But, in that
arid, smoke-filled Hades, so far from their time being
'almost death' and their 'dawns as faint as cracks on mudflats of despair', I was to catch again and again echoes of
that 'still sad music of humanity' which, blessedly, all
people resigned to their place in life may hear. Derelict as

they were, often friendless and alone, living out their moth-ball lives in cheerless bedsits, yet somehow they managed to raise many a good laugh and to raise my drooping spir-its many a time, by pushing out to the margins those mind-less routines that go by the name of honest work.

So I leave the place and that is that. The women give me a little party on my last day; there is tea and cake, a few bottles of wine even; and, for all their menace and frigid-ity, the starchy Lorigan and the jittery Rumpelstiltskin join in. When it is all over, I shake hands with them; and, quick as he came, the bird has flown.

The story should end there but it does not. For one day, years later, I walk into a café in the city and who do I find there sitting at a table near me but the most-important-man-in-the-world, the Chief.

Remarkably, he still has the same benign and ruminant face, and does not look all that much older. How could he when, at eighteen, anyone over the age of forty is an ancient? I go over to him and introduce myself. He looks up at me out of startled, bleary eyes and says he cannot place me.

'There were so many of you over the long years', he explains. 'All fine young fellows and girls. Most of them stayed but some left – for whatever reason I could never make out. Our Department was such a fine place, like one big happy family we were. For the life of me, I could never understand why any of you ever wanted to leave.'

I did not attempt to enlighten him. How could I when *he* was the head of the family and, once they all did his bid-ding, life was perfect? How could I possibly explain that, for this eighteen-year-old, their life was 'almost death', their dreams 'as faint as cracks on mudflats of despair'? It is not something you can say to someone who was once head of 'one big happy family'. And, on top of that, the most-important-man-in-the-world.

The Anthill

Do you recognise the initials V.K.? You should. They are the initials of a man of importance. Important to you, to the people next door to you, to everyone up and down your street. They have been looking at them for over forty years ... V.K. Victor King, a name of importance in the world.

It has a ring of importance to it, has it not? Concentrate for a moment, jog your memory a little, try to remember: think of receipts, a certain green receipt which comes through your letter-box at the end of each month; it has initials at the bottom right-hand corner, has it not? 'V.K.' – you remember now? I thought you would. Now, you can understand why I say they are the initials of a man of importance: initials that are known, not in a hundred, nor a thousand homes, but in hundreds of thousands of them up and down the length and breadth of this fair land. Shops, schools, factories, barracks, brothels, nunneries, everywhere, literally everywhere, they are known – the initials of the man who writes receipts. Without those initials, the receipts would be invalid; without a valid receipt, the system would not work. Homes and hospitals would close, workshops and factories too; trains and buses would stop; planes would not fly; the wheels of industry would cease to turn. The tenacity with which I, and my staff here in Receipts Division, keep signing them is a guarantee that civilised life, as we know it, will go on.

For fully forty years this has been my sole work. The cash, cheques, money-orders come in, and the receipts go out – forty years of a happy, fulfilled, well-contented life. It is the exception these days to find anyone above the age of twenty who hasn't a gripe or a grievance against some-one or something. For one, it's too little money; for another it's too much – for then, he complains, he has too much tax to pay. With another still, it is a house he wants but cannot afford; with another again, it is a house he can afford but must sell because he wants to own a better one. You will hear none of this nonsense from me. I have done something with my life. When my time comes, I shall have nothing to answer for but that I lived, worked hard, ini-tialled thousands and thousands of receipts. That is my story, my saga, my testament before the world.

'Victor King,' I shall say when the time comes for me to go, 'from the first day when you came to Receipts Division at eighteen years of age until the last when you left at sixty-five, you gave yourself, body and soul, heart and head and mind, to this vital national work. You served it unflinch-ingly without doubt or hesitation, gave it pride of place before all else in your life. Now, go in peace. May the Lord reward you.'

Be in no doubt of it, in these free-fall times, such dedica-tion on the part of a public servant is not appreciated. I have been the butt of jokes, have been laughed and snig-gered at and made fun of behind my back. Amongst the bright young things who are my subordinates here, I became known as 'King-of-the-kids'. Let them, I say; they can laugh all they like, I know what is behind their laughter. Envy, that's what's behind it. I am older, I should be less active: but still I can out-top them all with my record of performance. Yes, we are in the same job, we do the same tasks, but on any given day I can outpace them with twice, three times, sometimes as much as four times the number of receipts they put through their hands. So they can call me 'King of-the-kids' all they like, I take no notice. I have found my role in life and do not need their approval. If, for a single moment, they think I will be put off by their idle chatter, they little know the man they are dealing with.

'We do not expect miracles,' the old Chief said to me on the day I arrived long ago. 'Three hundred receipts a day is our average. We'll be pleased if you do more but you must try not to do less. Go ahead now, let's see what you can do for us.'

Three hundred – the poor old Chief! Within a week, I was doing 500, within a month 1,000. What's more, I loved it. From the first word, it had become the ruling passion of my life. Receipts, receipts, receipts, day by day I ate, drank and slept them. In the morning when I woke, I was up first thing and away to the office to tackle that day's quota. Often, before the day started at all, I was thinking about them: the slim green counterfoils falling thick as snowflakes all about me. So much so that one day the Chief, seeing the man he had, called me into his room and said something I have never forgotten:

'King,' he said, 'when you get to heaven, they'll have this monster Receipt Book just for you alone. And the faithful departed will not be able to come fast enough to keep up with you filling it in.'

A memory, alas, which is not without a sting in its tail. For, in the many years that have passed since it was said – and later again, when I was promoted to step into the old Chief's shoes – I regret to say that it has never once been my pleasure to say the same to anyone else. Indeed, if the truth be told, such things as I have had to say have been of a very different kind.

Let me tell you about one such incident which happened here the other day. It was with this insolent young fellow I had been keeping an eye on – a feckless, slovenly, indifferent eighteen-year-old, with no work ethic, no commitment to the job, nothing to recommend him at all. Whenever I checked on a receipt book he had done, I found blunders all over the place. I do not regard myself as an unreasonable man, but there is no way one can run an important Division like Receipts with work like that. So I took him aside and asked him to explain himself. Do you think an explanation was forthcoming? Or that I got a civil answer? Or a word of apology? Or a promise to make amends? You will scarcely believe me when I tell you what I did get.

NOTHING – that is what I got! Me, his supervisor, his Chief, a man with the power of life and death over him – and he offers me no excuse, no apology, for his whole lamentable performance, nothing, except to say that he is – UNHAPPY!

'Unhappy, my dear young chap,' I say to him. 'How can you be unhappy? You have a good job, a steady job, a job writing receipts. How can you be unhappy when you have a job like that?' Then, noticing his pale face and bloodshot eyes, I decide to pull back a bit. Perhaps something else is the matter? He may be going through a rough time perhaps? Maybe his health is not good, or he has debts which he cannot pay? Or, again, maybe it's a woman – you can never tell what these young bucks are up to these days.

'You can be quite frank with me,' I tell him. 'I am not your Chief, I am your friend. As you and all the staff in Receipts Division know, my door is always open. So, tell me now, you can be quite candid with me – are you having other difficulties?' No, he assures me, he is having no other difficulties at all.

'Well then, why is your work so deplorably bad? Can you offer me any explanation for that?'

'It's this place,' he tells me. 'This office, this job, this writing receipts.'

'And what,' I demand of him, 'is the matter with writing receipts that you should take it into your head to be unhappy with it?'

'I'm not just unhappy with it,' the young blackguard has the cheek to tell me. 'I hate the sight of it, it's driving me mad.'

By now, as you may appreciate, my blood pressure is rising. Whatever restraint I have been able to muster up to this has begun to desert me.

'Listen now to me, young man,' I tell him straight out, 'and take good heed of what I am saying. I have had quite enough of this nonsense from you. For forty years of my life, I have worked in Receipts Division. Forty years writing receipts – and still this hand of mine has not grown tired of it. Millions of them I have written and am still writing them. If you think you can stand there and tell me that what I have spent my life at is driving you mad and hope to get away with it, you have another thing coming.'

I stop, not because I have no more to say, but because I am so furious I cannot say it. My pulse is racing, my breath is coming hard. At my age, that sort of thing can be trouble. But do you think that mattered to this young buck? Or that what I said made the slightest impression on him? His sole response – the cheek of it makes my blood boil! – is to say that he is SORRY!

'Sorry?' I challenge him. 'Is that all you have to say?'

'I'm sorry I cannot be like you,' the brat persists. 'If I was, then I might be able to be happy like you. But I'm not and don't want to be.'

'And why not, pray?'

'Because writing receipts is not my idea of a happy life.'

'What is your idea of a happy life then?'

'Not writing receipts anyway. Some people may like that, I don't. It's like ants.'

'Ants?'

'Yes, ants. Ants like building anthills, that's their nature. It's the only thing they know how to do.' Despite my well-known self-control, this is the last straw. I feel the blood pounding in my temples, my breath is choking.

'Are you suggesting, young man, that I am an ant?'

'Oh, it's just a manner of speaking. An analogy.'

'A – what?'

'An analogy. Comparing something with something else to simplify its meaning.'

'Like comparing me with an ant?'

'Not quite. It's more like . . .'

'It's more like nothing. Get out. You're fired.'

You may guess that, by then, he had pressed me beyond my breaking point, my self-control was in tatters. I can neither stand nor sit. Up and down I go, pacing the floor like a caged animal. I would surely do myself harm if something could not be found quickly to soothe me.

I call to the outer office for a fresh book of receipt forms. When it is brought in, I finger the counterfoils for assurance, their clear, clean edges a balm to my shattered nerves. Within an hour, I have completed 200, within two I am up to 500, the initials 'V.K.' and the official stamp at the bottom right-hand corner of every one. By the time the staff begin to leave, I have completed the whole book. I call for another and it is brought in to me. I hear them go, laughing and chattering to each other; they seem glad to be getting away. What vacant, pointless lives some people live!

It is dark by the time I finish. The outer office and the streets beyond are silent. In the single light above my desk, there, in the out-tray before me, stand two tall columns of freshly completed receipts. Am I not entitled to feel proud?

I take my hat and coat and lock the door behind me. Out on the street, an anonymous person I may seem to be, one, just one, of that vast multitude who make up the body politic. But I know the truth. For am I not 'V.K.', Victor King, a man who makes the world go round? A truly happy, a fulfilled, a well-contented man.

A Feast of Tap-mites

It had all come out of so simple a thing as – thirst. Mr Crumm was thirsty: it was a hot summer's day, you or I might have felt the same. So he goes to the tap to fill himself a glass of water. He turns it on, lets the water flow for a second or two, then holds the glass out under it. Suddenly comes a tiny splash and – blimp! – there it is, The Thing, in the glass before him.

'Horrible, horrible!' he cries, revolted. Instinctively, he is about to dash it from the glass and let the water carry it down the drain and away when, abruptly, his sense of civic responsibility comes into play.

What if this Thing, this insect, this ugly and insolent creepy-crawly – it turns its back on him the moment it comes into his life and begins to wriggle its legs as if it doesn't care a fig for him and his sense of civic responsibility – what if it had come down the tap to someone else? Someone less spirited, less conscientious, less civically responsible than him? There are thousands, indeed millions, of such people about, the world is full of them. What, Mr Crumm asks himself, would they have done if they were in his place?

127

In all probability, they would have done what they always do – nothing. Just curse the town and its water supply, grumble to the family and tell the neighbours about it, and then promptly forget the whole thing. Some might not even go that far, some might not even notice it at all. Just drink the water, swallow it down, Thing and all – and let the town authorities go on as they were going, lazy and negligent in their bureaucratic arrogance, pouring contaminated water into the unsuspecting townsfolk.

'By Jove,' the high-minded, self-righteous Mr Crumm swears, 'they shall not do so to me.'

He takes an empty jar from the shelf and pours the incriminating evidence in. The occupant, momentarily stunned by this sudden rude propulsion into a new world, soon regains its calm and begins paddling about, indifferent to him and his lofty concerns. It will not remain indifferent for long.

Crumm takes the lid of the jar and jams it tightly shut.

'That fixes you, my friend,' he informs it. 'Tomorrow, you and I will be making a call.'

The man in the Water Analyst's office in the Town Hall is busy when Crumm goes in. He is a pale, timid man, balding, with a thin smile which Crumm at once interprets as a sign of weakness. But he is astonished by the man's first reaction when he is handed the jar, which is not one of weakness.

'My dear Mr Crumm,' he exclaims delightedly, 'that's quite a bloke you have here!'

'Quite,' Crumm replies frostily.

'You must feel . . . eh . . . quite . . . eh proud of him?' It is seconds only since they have met but already Crumm has begun to conceive a distinct dislike for this man; and already he has had quite enough of his idle pleasantries.

'Sir,' he arrests him sternly, 'you appear to be labouring under some kind of misapprehension.'

'A misapprehension, Mr Crumm? I don't understand.'

'Well then, let me enlighten you. The object you are holding in your hand – and examining, if I may say so, with such evident delight – arrived down the tap in my kitchen last night into a glass of what purports to be clean drinking water. The water, correct me if I am wrong, is supplied by the authorities of this town. What would have happened had I not had the good fortune to see what was in the glass before drinking it?'

The balding man seemed at a loss to know what the answer to this question might be. But, with Crumm breathing furiously beside him, an answer he must surely give.

'I suppose you might have drunk it?' he ventures.

'Precisely. And, in all probability, by now be either very sick or very dead.'

'Surely not, Mr Crumm? Not from a thing the size of that?'

'Surely yes. Things the size of that have killed people before now, they have killed whole populations in fact. Yet you have the effrontery – the brazen effrontery indeed – to stand there and suggest that in some way I should feel proud of it. Let me tell you, my good man, that the emotion of pride was very far from the feelings I did have.'

'Oh,' said the Analyst's man, suitably rebuffed, 'I see.'

'You may well say "I see". But what I have come here to discuss is not my feelings but yours.'

'Mine? But I'm afraid I don't have any. At least none that would have any bearing on a Thing like that.'

'Oh, you haven't, have you? Well then, let me do you the service of giving you some. That Thing was there because you people haven't been doing your job.'

'Not doing our job, Mr Crumm?'

'This is the Town Analyst's office, is it not?

Yes, the man timidly confirmed, this was indeed the office of that eminent personage.

'And it is your job to see to it that the town's water supply is clean?'

'We certainly check it regularly for impurities.'

'And do you mean to tell me that that Thing is not an impurity?' Crumm jabs angrily at the jar with his fore-finger. The Thing within, slumbering peacefully through the furore, is momentarily stirred to life by this sudden commotion. It wobbles about a bit, then sinks to the bottom of the jar, where it promptly proceeds to fall asleep once more.

'Of course, it's an impurity. Any fool can see that.'

'Are you calling me a fool, sir?'

'Not at all, not at all, my dear Mr Crumm. It's only a manner of speaking. The point, so far as I am concerned, is that there is nothing *bacteriological* about its impurity. I mean, you don't need a microscope to see a Thing like that.'

Crumm, a man not slow to anger or normally calm of mood, is now quite red with rage. The Analyst's man, momentarily roused from his normal torpor, is as near to rage as he will ever get. In a word, it is a confrontation rich in possibilities. Meanwhile, in the jar between them, The Thing wobbles and shakes its legs, tendrils or whatever they may be, a pacifist's plea for calm.

'I am sorry, Mr Crumm,' the man says, 'but I'm afraid you may have come to the wrong Department.'

'This is the Town Analyst's Department, is it not?'

'Yes, but as I have told you, we deal only with bacteri-ological pollution. What you appear to want is the Water-works Department.'

'Very well,' Crumm snaps, snatching the jar from the man's desk and stalking out. 'Be assured that I will not let this matter rest.'

At the Waterworks Department, he is met by a very differ-ent type of man; a man, this time, with a deep voice and an even deeper sense of gravitas. The gravitas is with respect to the job he does, a job which becomes markedly more important when Crumm suggests that he is not doing it.

Did he, the man growled, for a moment think that they in Waterworks were not aware of the facts of life? That water, coming from mountain and meadow, can do so without the risk of getting Things in it? Did he further think that, with the whole wealth of technical knowledge and expertise they had at their disposal, they hadn't made suitable provision for such matters? Had he ever, he asked, warming to his subject, heard of systems of water filterage and why they had been invented? Or was he perhaps one of that numerous and carping public, which emerged on radio and television as 'Vox Pops', who totally ignore the value of such systems or, worse still, think they were invented for fun?

Confronted with an even more brazen effrontery than he had encountered in the Town Analyst's Department, Crumm makes a mighty effort to control himself.

'What you say, sir, may be true,' he says in measured tones. 'But, as you and I perfectly well know, systems can go wrong, be they systems of water filterage or anything else. For example, it occurs to me, a mere layman I admit, that that Thing could have grown from spawn inside the filter beds; and, in that way, got through into the public supply.'

'Never,' the man summarily denies. 'Such a thing simply could not happen. The sand on the top layer of the beds has a very fine mesh, as fine as a piece of close-woven gauze. It is stripped off and put through a sterile rinse twice a week. How could a Thing of that size get through when something the size of the head of a pin could not?'

By now, he is on the point of losing his temper with this truculent intruder and showing him to the door. But he is a public servant and Crumm is a member of the public he is meant to serve. Furthermore, a recent in-house PR manual has laid emphasis on the need to treat members of the public with care and courtesy at all times.

Crumm, however, is under no such duress; add to this that, standing upon his civic rights, he detects in this man's combative response a further proof of bureaucratic cheek and insolence.

'So I am a liar then?' he challenges, his former choler quickly reviving. 'What you are saying is that that Thing could not have come out of my tap?'

'No, sir, you are putting words into my mouth. I did not say that at all.'

'But you implied it, which in my book is the same thing. You as good as told me that that Thing coming out of my tap did not come from your water supply. Let me inform you, my good man, that before you are many days older, you shall know better than to call my word in question.'

It is Crumm's misfortune to be a persevering man. A less persevering one would have gone under, would have allowed his anger to cool and his rage to evaporate in threats and curses and idle execrations. But he is not that sort of man. He is upright, civic, conscientious, responsible, all the things a man of principle should be. When he puts his mind to a task, there is no power in heaven or on earth that will shift him.

At the Town Hall, he asks to be shown to the Chief Clerk's office. When he gets there, it is to be told that the Great Man is engaged and, in any case, may never be seen without an appointment. His secretary, a young man with a ruddy face and buck-rabbit teeth, politely inquires whether, in his master's absence, there is not something he can do.

'Indeed there is,' Crumm tells him, producing the jar. 'You can inform your superior that last night this Thing came down the tap in my home from his town water supply.'

'What? A jam-jar?' Buck-rabbit asks, incredulous, as a good public servant should be, at the sight of such unruly wonders.

'No, not the jar – this!' Crumm says testily, jabbing at the jar, yet again disturbing its cat-napping inhabitant.

'Oh my, but the Chief will be pleased,' he is told. 'He's a regular expert on these Things, how did you know? Just daft he is about anything to do with insects – spiders, flies, arachnids, all such forms of insect life. He will be pleased.'

Delighted to be able to enrich a member of the public with this piece of personal biography on the part of his superior, he holds the jar up to the light, the better to see its singular occupant. It is a look full of curiosity, not unmixed with admiration. His Chief has told him more than once that the way to success in public life is to observe what your master says and does and, when your time comes, to say and do likewise. It is a lesson he has taken to heart. His Chief, noting this, has told him he is a young man who will go far.

'I'm afraid he has appointments for the rest of today, Mr Crumm,' he apologises. 'But I will certainly tell him you were here and will call to fix an appointment for you to come and see him soon.'

A day passes, two, three and no call comes. Meanwhile, Crumm drinks water from the tap each day, as his nature requires; but he does not do so without examining minutely each glassful for any sign of a recurrence

There is none. He scarcely dares admit it but, secretly, he is displeased: just one more Thing, even a tiny one, tinier even than The Thing itself, that would do. How much more justified in his indignation could he then feel! But, each time, the glass is clear and he drinks it down, a man with a cause against the civic powers now about to be robbed of his cause. At last, on the third day, the call comes. Though three days have elapsed since he was in the Town Hall, his ire has not abated; he is still the same Crumm, the man of principle who will not allow an arrogant bureaucracy to prevail.

Significantly, the moment he arrives, he is shown upstairs to the top administrative suite where, behind a mahogany desk, sits the Chief Clerk; a desk from which all else has been removed but the jar with the abominable Thing within.

'First, let me apologise for the delay in seeing you,' the Chief says smilingly. 'But pressure of business and all that. It's the old story, I daresay you know all about it yourself.'

Yes, Crumm acknowledges, he knows about it alright; but pressure of business is not what he is here to talk about.

'I see you have the jar,' he says, coming swiftly to the point.

'Indeed I have, Mr Crumm. And let me be the first to congratulate you on your find.'

Crumm's frosty face goes stiff with disbelief.

'My find?'

'Indeed, Mr Crumm. Upon your find – and your singular good fortune.'

He rises from his chair and comes forward, his hand outstretched.

Crumm, mystified, declines the handshake.

'I do not understand, sir. Will you kindly explain what it is you are talking about?'

'But surely you understand, surely no explanation is needed? This is quite an extraordinary Thing you have here. My secretary has told you, has he not, about my life-long interest in such Things. So, from my point of view, it is quite providential that you did not swallow it. I mean, if you had, consider the loss.'

Crumm, invited to consider the loss, considers instead whether the man is all there. Behind his small gold-rimmed spectacles, sharp green points have begun to dilate.

'The loss? What loss? I was as good as dead, sir, if I had not had the good fortune to see that Thing before swallowing it. And you say – consider the loss.'

'Yes, yes, of course I see your point,' the Chief brushes aside the objection. 'My secretary told me about your concern. In the circumstances, I daresay I might have felt the same myself until I contacted the Natural Life Museum people earlier today and they came over to have a look. Oh-ho, my dear Crumm, but had we them then guessing! It isn't every day of the week they get so rare a species of tap-mite in this part of the world. There may even be an award. There will certainly be a citation – with your name on it, in one of the public showcases.'

If Crumm is left speechless by this piece of intelligence, it is because no words he could utter could express the thoughts that were in his mind; but there is more to come.

For, in the days when bureaucratic delay had kept it waiting, The Thing has most ungallantly gone and died; and lies now, belly-up – if in so minute a creature a belly could be discerned – a tiny defunct mound clouded in a fog of its own mould at the bottom of the jar.

'What a pity,' the Chief Clerk sighs, taking it from the table and holding it up to view. 'But we must not lose hope. It seems there is a chance, not much of a chance the Natural Life people warn me, but there is still a chance that, since this one came down, there may be others. There is even a chance, they tell me, that there may be whole nests of them.' Hearing this, Crumm recalls all the glassfuls of water he has drunk from the tap since this verminous and abominable creature entered his life.

'Nests?' he weakly repeats.

'Now, now, Mr Crumm,' the Chief hastens to calm him, 'we must not be too hopeful. It's only a chance. The danger, I'm told, is that in the meantime the spawn may have run away.'

'What spawn?'

'Its spawn. You wouldn't have seen it of course, it would be too minute – and quite invisible to the naked eye.'

With that, he picks up the jar and hands it to Crumm, turning upon him a look of mute condolence. Upon which, he notices that, for some unaccountable reason, that ruddy and choleric gentleman has suddenly begun to go pale.

Out of Touch

Friday was a bad day for old Ned. It was the end of the week, payday for most people, including himself – when *he* had a job. He saw them now crossing Butt Bridge, men and women with warm houses to go home to and enough money in their pockets to keep them that way; enough too, for any of them that way inclined, for a pint or two in Kennedy's beside the bridge before catching the outbound train from Tara Street station. Well, that was the way of the world: for some, full and plenty; for others, nothing at all – like himself, leaning over the parapet of the bridge, watching the Liffey flow by and the dregs of his own life flow with it. Wednesday would be his next date with destiny: that was doleday, when he went to the paw-marked hatch in the Labour Exchange to collect his weekly stipend against destitution.

Small as it was, it brought back a brief, blessed sense of independence. He liked the jingle of coins in his pocket and the feel of the crisp new notes as he headed off to shop or supermarket where they swiftly parted company once more. By Friday, both money and independence were gone;

136

it was pinch-and-scrape then over the long weekend and the even longer days after the weekend until the next dole-day came around.

It need not have been so. A few years back, he had been made redundant in Macferran's Builders Suppliers Yard and was given two options: a lump sum or a small weekly pension. The pension would have cut his Social Welfare money, so he took the lump sum instead, £5,000 into his fist – what could a man in the whole of his health not do with that! A small cigarettes and sweets shop out Fairview way was what he had in mind, where he would keep a variety of household lines for sale as well; things he could handle without too much difficulty to bring him the modest profit that would keep him for the rest of his days. Give him a few months at the business, a year at most, and he would be right back where he started, only better – not a weekly mendicant on Social Welfare, but a man in full employment, with an independent means of livelihood, all his very own. And, what was more, having paid the initial deposit on the shop's rental, he would have the rest of the £5,000 tucked safely away in a Post Office Savings Book.

In a word, he would be a snug and happy man.

But the weeks passed as he dithered and hesitated; there were constant delays and differences about the lease and the rental; in the meantime, he had to live on something. In any case, plans come easy but actions do not; and, in short, it seemed no time at all until there was nothing left in the thumb-marked Savings Book but a blank line where the figure £5,000 used to be.

From then on, it was come-day, go-day, God-send-Wednesday, a jaded and joyless rigmarole of a life, with no silver linings to brighten the future anymore. This was the state he was in when he looked up from the parapet of the bridge one day and saw his old workmate, Peter Dorgan, coming towards him.

It was the peaked cap and curved pipe that caught his eye: Dorgan once told him that those were the first two pieces of apparel he put on every morning! Neither that nor anything else about him seemed to have changed over the years: a solid citizen was Peter Dorgan, with his jaw clenched firmly on the pipe, his step the step of a man who knew where he was going.

'Glory be to God, if it isn't Peter Dorgan himself,' old Ned exclaimed with genuine pleasure. 'How is every bit of you, old friend?'

Dorgan looked at him, the quick sceptical look one might give a professional toucher. But quickly he saw how wrong he was – this was no toucher, but Ned Kelly, a man he had known all his working life.

'I'm fine, Ned, and I'm glad to see you're looking well too. We had no word at all of you since you left Macferran's what is it, five years ago? What have you been up to all this time?'

Ned looked at him from under the greasy rim of his shapeless hat. The man was older, his hair was white above the ears; like Ned himself, he had probably gone bald above that again but, with the cap down on his forehead, that wasn't showing. That said, he still looked the same Peter Dorgan he had always looked, a man full of a quiet dignity, something Ned had always admired. Right then, he couldn't help thinking what a contrast he was to himself: with the lump sum well gone, what was he but a feckless, washed-up old has-been, whatever optimism and high hopes he had once cherished long since spent? There was no doubt in his mind what Peter Dorgan would do when his time to leave Macferran's came: there would be no quick-trick lump sum for him, no cloud-cuckoo-land of a cigarettes-and-sweets shop; it would be the pension, the steady regular thing, week by week, and no love-on-the-dole at the end of it.

For him, there would be no gazing into the Liffey across the parapet of Butt Bridge on Friday evenings, as the crowds went home, leaving him like some dried-up hulk with the tide gone out, its future, like its past, behind it.

The siren of the train approaching Tara Street station cut in across their conversation.

'That'll be my train,' Peter Dorgan said, making ready to go. 'I'll tell you what, Ned. Let's not leave it so long until we meet the next time. Why don't we make it a regular thing – say, here at the same time next Friday? We might even have a drink in Kennedy's, what do you say? There's only a few of us left and none of us is getting any younger.'

That would be fine with him, old Ned agreed. So they shook hands and parted but when he took his hand away, there was a little ball of paper in it, a rolled-up five-pound note.

The following Friday, and every Friday after that, he stood at the corner of the bridge and waited. And each time his old workmate came along and did the same thing. He should have felt bad about that and, in a way, he did; but beggars can't be choosers; so he swallowed his pride and took the money without demur. Pride is one thing but you cannot eat, drink or smoke it. Now, he could indulge himself with the odd twenty Gold Flake or pint of Guinness on Friday night without feeling that he would have to go without his bit of fast food the following day. It wasn't much, but to him it was everything. In spite of what he had increasingly begun to feel over these past few years, he was coming around to the idea that maybe there might be a God in heaven after all!

But then, one Friday, Peter Dorgan did not come. Ned waited and waited, the sirens hooted and the trains came and went, the home-going commuters going along with them. Still, he stood there at the corner of the bridge, hoping – in spite of himself, even praying – that the familiar sight of the peaked cap and curved pipe would be the next thing he would see; but it never was. Soon, the rush-hour was over and the crowds thinned out. There were longer intervals between the trains, the traffic came in shorter, more sporadic bursts. Each time, when the lights changed and the latest flow went by, the place became even quieter than before. At last, he gave up and went home.

Three, four, five Fridays after that, he waited, his ravelled sleeves resting on the bridge parapet, watching the world go by. What else was there for him to do? Maybe the man was sick, maybe he had gone on holidays, maybe it had slipped his mind for a spell and he had taken to going home some other way? If that were so, there was always a chance that he would come by next week. People said there was no stress once you had retired and left the cares of a daily job behind; but, for old Ned, in all his years he had never remembered stress like this: waiting and watching, hoping against hope that the next face he would see would be the face of his old friend. It was a vain hope. Could it do any harm to strip one more layer from the thin covering of his threadbare pride and go and seek him out?

The foreman in Macferran's was a brisk young man in a white coat, with a mobile phone stuck to his ear. This, with the way he first looked at him and then ignored him, made it plain that he was not in a mood to be distracted; certainly not by some unkempt straggler who had wandered in casually off the street. Old Ned touched his hat deferentially as he shuffled up to him.

'I'm busy, can't you see?' the man snapped. 'Did you want something?'

Ned told him who he was and how he had worked in the timber yard all his life until they retired him some years before.

'That would be before your time, of course. You're new here.'

'Not that new,' was the curt response. 'You wouldn't know many of the people around here now.' Looking about him, old Ned agreed: for one thing, there were women, lots of them, girls mostly – there was none of that in his time. Of the few men about, not as much as a single face did he recognise.

'Some of these were hardly born when I worked here,' he laughed thinly. 'Maybe inside in the inner yard I might do a bit better?'

The foreman checked him abruptly with a raised hand. Ned saw the rebuff but went on.

'I don't want to intrude. It's just that I wanted to have a word with an old friend.'

'What friend?'

'A man I used to work with here. He used to be foreman in the inner yard in my time. Peter Dorgan.'

'An old chap with a peaked cap and a curved pipe?'

'That's the man.'

'Didn't you know?'

'Know what?'

'He's dead. Died a month ago.'

Old Ned lifted his hat and for a moment went silent. Then, walking away, he said:

'God rest him, he was one hell of a decent man.'

The foreman looked at him frostily, a look that did not give the impression that he was in sympathy with what he had been told.

'Was he then? I wonder was that what brought him in here on Fridays long after we retired him, cadging around among the old hands for a few bob? For a friend in need, he used to tell them. They all suspected who the friend was – himself. These ould fellas have such a cunning way with them. We had to give him the bum's rush in the end, he just kept getting in the way. Ould fellas like that are so out of touch with the world we're living in now.'

The Hidden Spring

Two years to the day it was since her sister, Ita, died. Florrie remembered it as if it were yesterday: white clouds scudding across the sky, seagulls wheeling and screaming overhead, and she standing there above the grave, vowing that whatever else her sister's husband, Maurice, and their two young daughters might lack, they would never lack for the care and attention she could give them.

There had been times since when that was not easy. She went on timeshare in the job, working nights, so as to be there for the little girls when they came home from school in the afternoons. Her sole break was when they went off with their father for a fortnight's holiday in August; but, with the house empty, that then became her spring-cleaning time, so as to have everything spick and span for them when they came back. Still, she did not regret it, not one tiny little bit. It was good to see how the children grew on her and she on them. When one of them fell and hurt herself, it was to her they ran rather than to their father; when something went wrong at school or when some of the other kids about the place were ruffling them, it was to her they always came with their complaints. That meant more work, more worry – but it also meant a kind of covert happiness, a happiness she had never known before.

Could it have gone on that way? Could all that quiet peace and harmony have continued, with nothing else in her life but Maurice and the children, nothing but them to look after for the rest of her days? She was a woman, a young woman still in her mid-twenties, didn't that matter? Didn't she want to have a man, a husband of her own, children too? Of course, she did – doesn't every woman? But that would have to wait; there was no time for it now, certainly not while the little girls were young and needed her around. As for him, what was he but a brother-in-law, a big brother by another name? Well, a girl doesn't go falling in love with her big brother, does she? Besides, at the age she was now, all that could be pushed off into the distant future. Whenever it happened, if it did happen, it would be time enough to think about it. In the meantime, what with her job in the insurance company and looking after the family, she had a life that was more than full.

And then this thing happened which changed all their lives. It was the day they came back from their annual holiday in his parents' place in west Cork, the usual second fortnight of August – her own spring-cleaning time. As she went through the rooms with duster and hoover during the days they were away, the house sounded hollow and empty, it was nothing at all without them. Now, they were back, bounding up the steps and banging on the front door, screaming and shouting as she let them in and they clung to her and hugged her.

'Florrie, Florrie, Florrie, it's great to be back. Look what we brought you.'

Cakes and chocolates came out and fresh country flowers with sprays of hawthorn through them; a lovely, wild, happy house it was then, with no shadow of death or sorrow or parting ever touching it at all. Some people, she

thought, keep their houses like showcases, all spit and pol-
ish, with everything exactly in the right place. She would
never be like that, not now anyway. Up and down the
stairs the little girls raced, in and out of bedrooms, pulling
open the drawers and flinging things about – the tiered
order of her two weeks' work laid waste about her and the
hollow, empty silence exploding on all sides. She loved it,
revelled in it; it was springtime, lovetime, the brawling
gusty days of spring, full of a rapturous sound and fury
after a long dark winter.

Just to be with them then, to have them back with her,
they and their father, sun-tanned and happy now after *his*
short break, that was all she would ever ask of life: to love
them, to have and to hold them, to tell them how glad she
was to be with them – yes, yes, yes, she could openly say
it: she was as happy as any real mother ever was or could
be, with her husband and children back home in their own
house with her. Or so she thought.

Later that night, after she had put the girls to bed, she went
back downstairs to the living-room where Maurice was
looking at television. He was never a talkative person and
tonight was no exception; but she felt that there was something unusual about his silence this time, as he looked at
her across the room: a look that seemed part fear, part
pain, moving like a shadow upon his face. Was she imag-
ining it? Was she creating anxiety for herself when there
was no cause for anxiety there? Upstairs, she could hear
the little girls chattering away to each other, still full of
excitement about their holiday and, even more, about
being back.

'Will you just listen to that pair?' she said, breaking the
silence. 'They're still full of chat about the times they had.
It must have been great fun for them.'

'Oh, they had a time of it alright,' he told her. 'What
with the freedom of being able to run wild about the place,

and the farm animals, and everyone dancing attention on them, they had the time of their lives.'

And you, she wanted to ask, what about you? What kind of a time did you have? It was on her lips but the words would not come. That same look she had noticed before was on his face and she wondered – what is it, what does it mean? She had the uncanny feeling that it meant something for her.

'How about yourself?' she ventured at last. 'How did it go for you?'

It seemed ages before he answered. When he did, she knew at once that her instinct was right.

'Fine,' he said. 'In fact, in some ways, too fine. I'd been waiting until things quietened down to tell you.'

'Tell me what?'

'I've got myself engaged.'

By turns, the sultry heat of the late August night and an icy cold gripped her. Got himself engaged – had she heard him right? Was this a dream, a nightmare? God, God, please let it be that! In a moment, she would wake up and open her eyes and it would be over. She would be upstairs in her own room, with him and the girls in their rooms across the landing, sleeping soundly until the alarm clock woke them, to the chatter of the birds in the beech trees outside the window and the start of a bright new day. But she was not dreaming. The reality of what he had said cut like slivers of ice through to the core of her heart.

She began to feel dizzy, as if she were about to faint. Feeling the weakness come over her, she put her head back against the headrest and shut her eyes.

'Are you alright, Florrie?' he asked, coming over and putting his hands on her shoulders. 'Have I upset you?'

'No, no,' she lied. 'It's just all the excitement of our family being back.'

It was out before she knew it. But, even if she could have stopped, she would not, for it was the truth: many times over the long months since her sister died, she had felt it – this *was* her family, the only family she would ever want; and he, her sister's husband, the only man she wanted in her life. In every sense but one, she had him; now that those telltale words had been spoken, she wanted him in that sense too. She could feel his hands on her shoulders through the light silk tee shirt. She longed to feel them more and more, wanted him to take her in his arms and hold her like any lover might hold his woman and, with love and kisses, tell her she was not just his dead wife's sister, but a beloved woman he wanted for herself alone. Would this be the only touch of his hands she would ever now know?

'I was afraid you might not take it so well,' he was saying. 'On account of Ita being dead only a few years and that. But this thing just happened, I didn't plan it or anything. She's a nice woman, Mai is, she likes the girls and they like her. When you meet her, I'm sure you will like her too.'

Fool, fool, she thought – what kind of a woman does he think *I* am? Like her, will I? How can I like her when, already, I hate her? Hate her as ever a rival 'other woman' was hated – for taking my life away, my children, my man, everything I love and own?

And yet was he any more of a fool than she was? Women are supposed to be the ones with the instincts, the intuition. Where were her instincts and intuition while she lived under the same roof with a man she had come to love, yet never once gave the slightest hint of it? Why, why under heaven, had she not done so? Bitterly, angrily, the truth came to her: it was because she did not know it herself. If she had, this other thing might never have happened. Instead, the thing she wanted most of all in the world might have; a thing that had been so near to her, but was now suddenly so far away?

'Don't cry, Flor,' he said, pressing his hands upon her shoulders. 'It need make no difference at all to us. We've discussed it, Mai and I – you're to stay on here in your own room. With the children around, it will be just the same as always. Only at least you'll have less work to do – in fact, you can go back to the daytime hours in the job again.'

For the Nth time in those devastating minutes, she wanted to scream 'Fool, Fool' at him: the only daytime hours she wanted were the ones her dead sister had left her with; now, so far from that being a burden, it was the only work she wanted for the rest of her life.

Could he not see that? Could he not see the tell-tale other signs: a young woman giving her whole life to him and his, joyfully, without complaint, with a trust and a willingness that only lovers can have? But no way could she bring herself to say such things to him now.

'I knew this would come as a bit of a shock to you,' he went on. 'On account of Ita especially. I'll say this much, if it's any help. It came as a bit of a shock to me too. I thought I had finished with all that after Ita died. But I was wrong. To tell you the truth, there were times in the past two years when I felt so alone that I thought I'd go mad. Please God, that's all over now?'

All over indeed, a savage jealous devil of feeling inside her thought. And, more savagely, bitterly still, the thought came: I hope it's not over at all. How else can *I* face the years to come, looking at him and his children, *my* family – a man I love, children I love – with a new wife, a new mother, when that wife, that mother, should have been me?

The Moons of Jupiter

For a brief period in my life I was an undergraduate in University College Cork, with English and Anglo-Irish literature among my subjects, a futile and unrewarding time as it happens. My real ambition was to get out of college as fast as I could and into the civil service, where I would have a fine, white-collar job to keep me for the rest of my days! Perhaps the only abiding memory I have from that time was a novel, *The Moons of Jupiter*, written by a lecturer there, one Desmond Cross.

It told the story of a young student in UCC up from the country and staying with his uncle in a fine house on the Western Road. The uncle's daughter, Irina – and so his own first cousin – was also there. She had just finished boarding school and would be with him in university the following year. She played the piano and sang, a voice as true and clear as a blackbird on a May morning. When the sound of her singing came up to him from downstairs while he tried to fix his mind on his books, it put an end to all concentration; he just sat there spellbound, the books open in front of him and his eyes on the page, but seeing or hearing nothing but her. He never dared to go downstairs then, never made the slightest noise or stir for fear she might hear him and stop.

Later, at mealtimes, when he looked at her across the table, this extraordinary feeling would come over him, a glow of tenderness which turned the whole world to gold. It took him a long time to see this for what it was: he was young, it was years ago, the ways of the world have changed a lot since then. But, even if he did know, he did not want to recognise the feeling or to accept it because of the terrible effect it would have – on her, on him, on the whole family.

Then, one night when he was out on the back lawn above the River Lee, looking at the stars mirrored in the water, he picked out the constellation known as 'The Moons of Jupiter'. As he did so, the sound of Irina's voice floated towards him across the night air. He went in and stood behind her; but, this time, though she heard and saw him, she did not stop. When she finished, he put his hands on her shoulders and she leaned back against him until her head rested on his chest. They stayed that way a long time, neither of them moving or saying a word. But in that time they both knew that something had happened, something which, being first cousins, took on a grave, unhappy significance in their lives.

Because, in those years, first cousins – like brothers and sisters – were within what the Church called 'the forbidden degrees of relationship'. This meant that, no matter what was between them, it could never come to anything more than friendship. The story finishes with her going off as a lay missionary to Africa, leaving him with his books and his 'Moons of Jupiter' to keep him company for the rest of his life.

The book came out in paperback some years later and this time, having left the civil service and, in the meantime become involved in writing, I was keen to find out how much truth there was in the story. By this time, Desmond

Cross had long since retired and was living in a remote corner of west Cork. When I rang to ask if I could come and see him, the directions I was given turned out to be quite confusing; but for the little old lady behind the grille in the village post office when I arrived, they would have been more confusing still.

'Oh, Mr Cross,' she said, peering at me above her gold-rimmed spectacles, 'we know him well around here. He lives along the cliff walk about a mile down the road. Comes in for the paper every morning, so he does. Very polite and reserved he is, him and his housekeeper, all alone in their hideout down there. They keep very much to themselves.'

She gives me directions and away I go. The hideout turns out to be an old cottage-style bungalow, standing on its own, covered in Virginia creeper and set far in beyond a line of tall eucalyptus trees. Thick leaves clogged the gateway and rooks cawed in the branches high above; an odd place for an old man to live, I begin to think: beautiful, yes, by all means, with nothing but the cliffs and the wild Atlantic out in front and the rich rolling hills of west Cork behind. But, by late August when the tourist season was over, the holiday homes all around shut their doors and were locked up for the winter; it would be fully nine months before there was a sign of life around the place again. Yet, the old lady in the post office told me, Desmond Cross and his housekeeper continued to live there right through the winter, two old and fragile creatures like a pair of gannets clinging to their ancient rock.

Beyond the gate there is this fuchsia bush in full bloom and, through it, I catch a glimpse in the window of the man I have come to see. He is, of course, older now than when I had last seen him; the mane of hair above his drooping head is snow-white and the spectacles are down on his nose. But I recognise him at once from his picture on the cover of the recent reprint of his *Moons of Jupiter.*

'Come on in,' he welcomes me, drawing open the front door. 'We were beginning to fear you were lost and might never find us at all.' I follow him into the small comfortable sitting-room where, on a window seat looking out towards the sea, a woman the same age as himself is sitting. Serene and quite remarkably beautiful she is, despite her age. She rises and bows to me in a shy deferential sort of way.

'Miss Devlin, my housekeeper,' he introduces her. 'We sometimes take a short walk down the cliff road these nights, once we know that the holiday crowds have gone. We thought we might meet you on the way. Only the sea-gulls and the rooks know their way up to this place.'

'But he's young, Desmond,' the old lady joins in, in a voice that has the ring of bells to it. 'Young people never have any trouble finding places, it's only us old folk who get lost.'

For the next few hours, we talk about many things, but mostly about books and writing, which is my reason for being there. Whenever he speaks, she remains attentive but says very little herself. Occasionally, she nods her head in acquiescence or shakes it as if to say that things had not been quite that way. When he pauses for a moment to rec-ollect something, she comes in at once, taking up exactly where he left off.

They seem to be a perfectly adjusted couple, closer to each other in thought and sentiment than most married people who have spent their whole lives together. But, when I try to get onto the subject that brought me here, the origins of *The Moons of Jupiter*, its author becomes strangely evasive.

'Oh, I'm afraid that all took place a long time ago,' he says noncommittally. 'I have more or less forgotten about it now.' This is followed by a silence when the only sounds I hear are the clinking of the teacups, the rooks and pigeons in the trees outside, and the waves pounding on the foreshore. Each time, when I try to bring the conversation back to the book, the old lady gets up and moves about the room, shifting and adjusting things, as if to distract attention. But, if I am to get anywhere with this inquiry of mine, I will have to do so soon; for, already, the light is fading, half an hour later it will be gone.

'What I am interested in is the origin of works of fiction,' I try again. 'What makes people write things, what basis in real life has an author or playwright to write a particular story or play. *The Moons of Jupiter*, for instance, was that pure imagination or was there something in real life that sparked it off?'

I am looking at him as I say this and see his face darken. The old lady moves quietly into the background. A silence follows in which I fear I may have lost him. But then a dry smile forms about his lips and I know I have not.

'I'll tell you – if you promise me not to put it in writing anywhere.'

That will be no problem, I assure him; I am here purely out of personal interest; whatever he tells me will not be repeated, nor will I write about it.

'Well, it was something quite simple really,' he begins. 'I was twenty and there was this girl I was fond of. I wanted to tell her but I couldn't; there was a reason but we needn't go into that. In any case, at that time – not like now – there was much greater reticence in talking about such matters. So I thought up the bright idea of putting it in the form of a book. Her twenty-first birthday was coming up, so I wrote the book for her as a means of telling her. In a sense, you could say that *The Moons of Jupiter* was a love-letter and a birthday present at one and the same time.'

It was a charming story, I thought, and said so. But I said one thing more which instantly changed the whole atmosphere of that serene and friendly place.

'She got a splendid birthday present, whoever she was. It's a fine book, with a core of truth to it that nothing, not even time, will ever change.'

That was all I said. Not much, was it? Yet, the moment I said it, a cold chill seemed to enter the place; and, when he spoke again, there was no doubting the edge in his voice.

'Oh, you're quite wrong about that, young man,' he told me. 'Things have changed alright and for the better too. Can you imagine a couple of cousins turning their backs on each other now because of some stupid Church rule about "the forbidden degrees of relationship"? Did you ever hear such bloody nonsense? Nowadays, they wouldn't even bother getting married, just live together and be happy, the same as any other couple. And let the busybody Church think whatever it likes.'

There was no doubting it, the atmosphere had changed alright. In that warm, comfortable room, with the waves pounding on the rocks below and the air filled with the hints of a delicate and sensitive past, something seemed to suddenly explode, an outburst that was as explicit as it was out of character with the two gentle people there.

The old lady began to fold her table napkin and gather up the tea things to cover the embarrassment. By then, the light had all but gone. The rooks settling down in their nests in the eucalyptus trees made small chattering sounds. Soon, it would be dark.

'You won't mind us not seeing you down to the gate?' she asks apologetically as I get up to leave. 'Our eyes are beginning to play tricks on us, especially at night. I do hope your journey was worthwhile.'

I thank her and we shake hands. When I look back over the trodden leaves, she is still there, waving to me from the front door. Then, through the hollow silence, I hear Desmond Cross' voice from within.

'Come on in, Irina, you'll catch cold.'

153

The door closes and I am alone. I stand there in the darkness, looking up at the night sky studded with stars, among
them The Moons of Jupiter. Then, faintly, above the cries
of the curlews and the seagulls out over the water, comes
the sound of a piano playing and a woman singing, in a
voice that has the ring of bells.

Quiet Saturday Afternoons

You have, of course, heard the old saying that 'high walls make good neighbours'? Well, for me, it was never proved to be more true than when we moved into our first house as newly-weds – a nice tidy little bungalow in a cul-de-sac, with fine gardens front and rear, something that has gone out of fashion entirely now with the mad property boom. As well as the gardens, there were wide entrances on both sides, giving plenty of room between one house and the next. But, however much room there was, it wasn't enough for two neighbours up the road who, we soon came to realise, needed a lot more than high walls to keep them apart.

This pair, Pat Irey and Mr Pim – their very names give a clue to their characters – had only just recently moved in but, within weeks, those of us who were already there could see that it would not take long for the spark to ignite. Unlike the other neighbours, they were both well-off, they had brand new cars in the driveways when the rest of us had old bangers, if even that, and they each sent their children to the best schools. In all these respects, they were similar; but in everything else, between Irey's idea of what to do with his money and his life and Pim's there was a wide gulf of difference.

Irey was brash, lavish and colourful; Pim was proper, economical and staid. They were about the same age but, age being a superficial thing anyway, there was in reality a whole generation of outlook, taste and lifestyle between them. Sooner or later, it was inevitable that it would come to a head.

Sooner was what it turned out to be. The day was fine, it was Saturday, and both were relaxing in their well-kept gardens after the strains and stresses of the working week. Sitting out on the patios with their wives they were when the air was suddenly rent apart by an explosion of sound. Mr Pim sprang to his feet as if he had been hit by a thunderbolt.

'What is it?' he asks his wife, who is basking on the deckchair beside him.

'It's music,' she says, somewhat unnecessarily.

'I know it's music,' he snaps at her, 'but where is it coming from?'

'It's from over there,' she tells him, pointing to the dividing hedgerow between the two gardens. Her husband goes to the hedgerow and looks through; and there, to his horror, in the window sill above his neighbour's reclining head, he sees a stereo, its volume turned up full.

This is where the generations of gentility and good breeding in which he has been reared come into play. Another man – a more direct, even a more neighbourly man – would have shouted at the top of his voice there and then at the rude intruder on the far side of the hedge to shut the bloody thing off, or at the very least to turn it down. Mr Pim was not such a man; by nature, his methods were more circumspect, his temper and mood more discreet. One must always practise restraint, he had been taught: good temper and good manners were the mark of the true gentleman. Besides, ignorant lout that this neighbour of his clearly was, in all probability there would be no point in shouting at him, which in effect would bring him down to the same level himself. Yet, neither was he going to sit there impotently and put up with the raucous assault.

In all such situations, the first thought in his mind was to consult with his wife. Like himself, she was a person of good breeding; but, like him too, she was nobody's fool when it came to being put upon by a neighbouring bully-boy.

'What are we to do?' he asks her. 'This is another of that fellow's crazy fancies, like the cabin cruiser in the driveway and the marquee on the back lawn. If I know anything about human nature, that fellow is going to cause trouble around here yet.'

His wife remains silent. It is a silence which, knowing her as he does, must not be mistaken for weakness. She had come from a musical family herself, where Saturday afternoons were often spent in the tuneful company of Gilbert and Sullivan wafting gently to them across the manicured lawn.

But that was a long time ago. Besides, it was very different from the 'music' she was having to listen to now. There was a further factor: she had a man in her life now, *this* man, a man with no music in his soul at all – certainly none of the kind that was shattering the neighbourhood peace. Clearly, something would have to be done about it. The 'something' would be done by her.

She goes indoors and switches on every electrical apparatus in the house; then, for good measure, she comes back out and switches on those outside it, including a power-drill in the toolshed which, she guesses, may be even more effective in creating major radio interference.

She guesses right. The effect of her intrusion on the cacophony from the far side is instantaneous. Irey jumps to his feet and rushes indoors at the first ear-splitting sound; and, what is more remarkable still, he does not come back out.

Which was the more deafening – the mad whirr-and-whine of Mrs Pim's gadgetry or the sudden stopping of the stereo – is a moot point. All one may assume is that that refined but canny lady is pleased with her deliverance. One by one, she goes about the place, switching the appliances off.

Her deliverance is short-lived. Ten minutes later, the music is back on; but this time, as she makes for the electrical apparatus to stop it, she looks out the window and sees a van with a complex of aerials on the roof and the words 'TV and Radio Interference Mobile Detection Unit' brightly blazoned on the near side.

What is to be done now? Clearly, this neighbour of theirs is not a man to be trifled with. And clearly, this time, he has outwitted them. But has he? She is not the determined wife of a determined husband to take this sort of neighbourhood bully-boy tactics lying down.

She goes to the toolshed and wheels out the power-mower, to which clamorous instrument she summarily directs her compliant man. Meanwhile, she herself takes out the strimmer and advances upon the dividing hedge. With consuming energy, the pair of them go at it, like coolies in the sun, the raucous concert of their labours battling it out for supremacy against the ghetto-blasted music from the far side. But the music continues and Pat Irey sits it out on his deck chair until, at last, the weaker side caves in. Discreet, polite, staid Mr Pim can stand the racket no longer; he buckles up under the weight of the joint cacophony and flees indoors. Seconds later, his wife follows him in.

'I know what you are thinking,' she says, sitting herself down on the couch beside him.

'What?'

'You're thinking of getting out.'

'Out? Out of what?'

'Out of here. You're thinking of selling up and getting out of this place?'

'I am and will,' the beaten man confirms. 'From the first moment I laid eyes on that fellow, I knew there was going to be trouble. One or other of us has to go, it's as simple as that. I'll ring the auctioneers first thing on Monday.'

His wife hears this news with trepidation. She knows her man and knows that, when he makes up his mind to something, there is no force in heaven or on earth that will stop him.

Though, with her at least, he is not normally a cussed nor a headstrong man, she knows that any attempt by her to dissuade him from his purpose now will serve only to inflame matters and make him more determined still. But it is her life as well as his; this is the house they bought after much heart searching; and here they are now being forced out of it by a loud and vulgar neighbour who wants to force his ugly tastes upon them.

'Why on earth should we do that?' she protests. 'He is the one who is causing the trouble. If anyone goes, it should be him. Maybe we should wait a while, brazen it out?'

'Brazen it out? What have you in mind?'

'It's perfectly simple,' she tells him. 'If he blasts us with his music, we blast him with ours.'

'What do you mean – ours?'

'Here,' she says, going to the CD-player. 'Help me to lift this out onto the patio.'

Mr Pim obeys. He always obeys when she is in this mood. Not that he is by nature an obedient man, certainly not where his wife is concerned; but there are times when the wisest course is to take counsel with another, especially when the other seems to know what he or she is doing. Besides – it is something he has noticed over the years – women can sometimes be inscrutably smart; and, when she takes it into her head, this woman can be smarter than most.

With the CD-player in place, she seeks out the disc she wants and puts it on. She fingers the volume button for a moment until the quiet opening chords are past; then, knowing the tumult of sound that is about to erupt, she turns the volume up full.

Her husband puts his fingers in his ears and looks towards heaven. Finding no respite for himself up there, he looks back down. When he does, he sees a remarkable sight: it is his wife standing beside him smiling benignly. Clearly, he feels, from now on things are going to be alright.

The music is Beethoven, the Choral Symphony, the most sublime music ever known to the mind of man. But for Mr Pim right then, the most sublime thing about it is that, the moment it starts, the clamour from the far side of the hedgerow stops. The space between the two houses is cut in half: on Pat Irey's side, the air goes stiff and taut with silence; on the Pims' side, the uncontested Beethoven pounds its hammer-blows upon the quiet suburban air.

Even nature itself sits up and takes notice as, from the beech and hawthorn trees behind the gardens, linnet, thrush and blackbird send up nervous, supplicating little cries.

Then, as rapidly as Irey's ghetto-blasting stops, another more menacing sound starts up. It is the sound of the Pims' outer gate flying open and of angry, aggressive footsteps approaching their front door. Mrs Pim goes pale, her pale husband goes paler. There is a loud knocking at the door, which leaves them in no doubt that trouble lies ahead. When Pim goes to open the door, there stands his neighbour – in a florid Hawaiian shirt and sweating profusely – but with his hand outstretched and a smile as broad as a billow on his face.

'We haven't met, old chap,' he says, thrusting the brawny paw into Pim's limp fingers. 'But let me say here and now how delighted I am to have a music lover for a next-door neighbour.' Pim is too shocked to utter a single syllable in response. His wife, bringing up the rear, thinks he may be in imminent danger of lockjaw.

'I have the distinct feeling that we two are going to be friends,' he goes on. 'I have a fine comprehensive set of records and CDs myself – Beethoven, Mozart, Brahms, the lot. What do you say – why don't we make it a regular thing, now that we know each other's tastes? Every Saturday afternoon from now on? You and your good wife, come on into us next Saturday. From then on, we can make it turn and turn about.'

Pim mumbles something about business engagements on Saturday afternoons as he steers his neighbour back to the outer gate. When he returns, he finds that his wife has left the Yellow Pages section of the Telephone Directory on the hall table; and has left it open at the page headed – Auctioneers.

Lucky Jim and Sue

Pat Irey and Mr Pim were not the only odd couple who inhabited that cul-de-sac of ours away back. There was a George-and-Mildred pair, an even odder couple; and, beside them, a Jim-and-Sue one, an innocent and unassuming little pair who had nothing much in the way of wealth in the world but who put everything they had to such splendid use that, to the casual observer, they were away ahead of everyone else.

This tale is about the George-and-Mildred pair, especially in their relationship with Jim and Sue. And, when I think about them, what comes out loud and clearest is Mildred's high-and-mighty voice,

I can do no better than let her do the telling and get out of the way myself. Put yourself in the mood for a hectoring, lecturing brave of the female species then, and this is what you might hear . . .

Rockfield House, my dears? Not at all, I hadn't the slightest idea a month ago that it even existed, not to mind that we would own it. Of course, we are thrilled, who wouldn't be? It's beyond our wildest dreams. Such an enormous place, seven bedrooms, five reception, and the kitchen – did I tell you about the kitchen? I'm still asking myself what I will do with all the space. Especially after being cooped up in the matchbox of a kitchen we had here – I don't have to tell you, you live here, you know. Remember what we used to say long ago when we came here first: that you couldn't swing a kitten in it, not to mind a cat. Well, you would swing a very big cat in the kitchen of Rockfield!! It's what I always say: a house can be any size you like but, for the woman, it has to have a good kitchen. It stands to reason, it's where she is most of the time.

Not that in Rockfield I'll be there all that much. Now that we have the space, George insists that I am to have a housekeeper. But talking gives you no idea. Why don't you come out and see it for yourselves? Come out and have dinner with us one night? Of course you'll be welcome, old friends, old neighbours. Will you have trouble finding the place, is it? Don't make me laugh, the minute you arrive, in Redbarn, Rockfield House will stand out. Our old neighbours across the road, Jim and Sue, are coming next Sunday – would you care to join them? You would? We'll be delighted. That will make six of us, it will be so nice having us all together again – you pair, me and George, Jim and Sue.

Isn't it odd the way they left here the same week that we did? It was no great surprise our leaving, we had been thinking and talking about it for months. But Jim and Sue – we thought they'd never leave after all the work they put into their little place here. There wasn't a thing more they could have done, just perfect they had it. As you well know, they're tiny, these little bungalows are, but that's where Jim and Sue shine. They don't seem to think in terms of space at all. Jim, of course, is the reason for that, he's such a fabulous craftsman. In their new place, he has done wonders already. You can talk about moving house when you're married to a man like that. Wouldn't be my George, I can tell you. George can't put a nail in the wall without pulling the house down.

They had us out in their new place last week. Mind you, it's still small and I won't say it's perfect, but give them a few more months and it will be. Between ourselves, we all know that Jim is only a junior clerk in that job of his, and they do have the three children. But they always manage to do things with such taste and style. Makes you wonder sometimes – maybe money isn't everything after all?

Needless to say, for sheer space and the exclusive residential area it's in, it doesn't bear mentioning in the same breath as Rockfield. Still, small is beautiful, they say. Just to give you an idea: Sue brought me up to see their bathroom. It has mirrors everywhere – on the walls, the floor, even on the ceiling. A little cubbyhole of a place it is in reality, but it looks huge. What's more, it gives the impression that the sun is shining there all the time. That's Jim for you. He may be only a junior clerk, but is he a masterhand when it comes to work like that! And then, to top it all, Sue tells me, he got the mirror glass as a job-lot, then cut and shaped it himself and did all the fitting. You wouldn't believe me if I told you how much it cost – it was next to nothing.

When I told my George about it, his reaction was typical. Knowing him as I do, I should have known what to expect. On your word of honour, my dears, you are not to repeat this to anyone. I wouldn't wish for the world that it got back to them. But I will say this: at the time, it did make me laugh.

'Like a pair of chimps in a cage they'll be,' he says, 'running around in their pelts in there for all they're worth. A bloody glass menagerie, that's what it is, if you ask me!'

Isn't he dreadful, my George? Of course, coming as he does from such a wealthy family, he hasn't any time for knick-knacks, only the solid, substantial thing. That's why Rockfield appealed to him so much. You should see the bathroom there! You may think I exaggerate, but the plain truth is that Jim and Sue's whole house would very nearly fit into it. And there is such luxury in space, don't you agree? Oh, I know they can't afford luxury like that. But then they don't need it, careful thrifty little folk that they are. Nothing astray, everything in place, nothing thrown away – that's Jim and Sue for you.

Let me tell you about the heating they put in. It's oil-fired but there are no radiators, can you credit that? Only fluorescent pipes recessed behind cowled skirting boards, it actually looks as if it's part of the lighting. But the miracle is that it gives heat and light at one and the same time. Again, George's reaction was typical. He says oil stinks; what's more, he says, that kind of heat is phoney.

'Phoney?' I say. 'What do you mean, phoney?'

'It's not real heat. For heat to be real, you've got to see where it's coming from. Otherwise, it's not heat at all.'

'Well, I don't know, George,' I say. 'But, for my money, heat is heat, no matter where it comes from.'

I mean, it's all very fine for him in his well-heated Director's office. He doesn't have to live in a huge freezing house all day. Oh, I know he's right when he says that Rockfield has great open fireplaces that would roast an ox – but heating like that went out with the flood. Do you think he takes any notice when I say that? It's no good talking to my George when it comes to things like heat. So far as he is concerned, the same fireplaces are a dream. And the fire surrounds that go with them are a marvel. In a way, it was they that sold us Rockfield in the first place. Because, believe me, for a time, I really did wonder whether we should go for it. Considering the size, the grounds, the grand scale of everything. And all for just the two of us. Even George saw the point when I made it – and he is not one to waver when he has made up his mind. That was when the auctioneer drew his attention to the fire surrounds.

'Genuine Adams they are, sir,' he told him. 'If ever you decide to sell, those fire surrounds alone could fetch millions.'

The moment he said it, I knew the deal was done. As I say, George has this great liking for the solid, substantial thing.

'Just feel the sheen on that stone,' he says, stroking the cool marble with the tips of his fingers. 'There's nothing ticky-tacky about that. Compare that with some cheap-jack's tricking about with bathroom mirrors.'

Impossible he is sometimes, my George. Can't you just see him in Jim and Sue's little place. After we left the night we were out there with them, I remarked on how lovely their entrance porch was, all done out in an off-white ceramic tile which made it look absolutely stunning.

'It's stunning alright,' George says, 'just like a bloody morgue. I think I might like it better if I was dead.' Small wonder he is 'Honest George' to his pals in the golf club. And, as if that isn't bad enough, then I happen to mention the kitchen. You see, Sue has all the services on one wall – fridge, dishwasher, spindryer, polisher, the lot – all clever-ly fitted together, with snow-white formica surfaces and rows of glass-front presses with cantilever doors at head-level above them. I thought it just fabulous, everything within easy reach in that tiny place. But that is not what George thinks at all.

'It looks like an operating theatre, if you ask me,' he says. 'You'd need a pair of rubber gloves and a face mask before going to work in there!'

In that particular case, he may, I admit, have a point. I mean, that sort of order suits some people – trim, orderly little people like Jim and Sue – but with George and me it wouldn't work at all. We just couldn't live that way, cer-tainly not now when we have settled into Rockfield. And yet, my dears, fine as it is, Rockfield is not without its disadvantages.

'What disadvantages?' George snaps, when I use the word on the way home from Jim and Sue's that night.

'Well, for one thing,' I tell him, 'the entrance hall is a bit on the dark side.'

'Dark side? What on earth do you mean?'

'Those mahogany floorboards,' I say. 'They're almost black.'

'That's genuine, seasoned mahogany,' he cuts me off. 'It's old world and dignified, in keeping with the style and tone of the house. The whole appearance and value of the place would not be the same without them. You're not suggesting for a moment that we carpet them?'

'Not quite,' I say. 'If we did that, the rain blowing in a squall the minute you open the front door would rot any carpet we put down in a month.'

'What do you suggest then?'

'Well,' I venture, 'what would make a wonderful improvement would be to have the whole entrance done in that nice ceramic tiling thing Jim and Sue have in their entrance porch.'

You can always tell when George doesn't warm to an idea. He goes dead silent, can't be got to say another word. But, now that I'm on the subject and have gone so far, I think that maybe I ought to go a bit farther.

'The kitchen too,' I say. 'That could do with a bit of improvement as well.'

'What improvement?' he retorts. 'I think it's perfect, I had the impression that you thought so too.'

'And so I did, but I've been thinking of a few things since.'

'What things?'

'Well, George dear,' I soothe him, 'it's huge, it has all the space we never had in our little bungalow here but, in a way, that's the problem.'

'What problem? I see no problem. Space was what you always wanted.'

'And so it is. But the trouble is that, in the Rockfield kitchen, everything I need is out of reach, it's miles and miles away. What would make a huge improvement would be to have all the services beside each other on the same wall – fridge, dishwasher, spindryer, polisher, the lot – with glass-fronted presses above them and white formica coverings on the working surfaces below.'

A funny thing, my dears, but from the moment I said that, George did not speak to me again the whole way home, nor for the rest of the night. He never even said goodbye to me when he went off to work the following morning.

What can I possibly have said wrong? Maybe he thought I was finding fault with Rockfield? And I wasn't, not really. How could I – it's such a magnificent place: such space, such substance, such fine old-world style.

A Man of Substance

And then there is Mr Brand, a stern name for a stern man. He lives in a large house set in its own grounds at the top of our cul-de-sac, a house with a strong teak gate which separates it from the rude world outside. It is at this very gate that the tale of Mr Brand's fall from greatness begins.

It is a brisk morning early in the new year when he comes out of his house and sits into his brand-new car. The car, a top-of-the-range Jaguar, is in keeping with the style and status of the man who owns it, for he is an important Director of an important business and nothing less will serve his sense of self-esteem.

He notes the white frost on the roofs of the lowly bungalows that surround him and notes, for recompense, how it glistens on the grass of his own mature and well-kept lawns. His little son, a ten-year-old boy, with ruddy cheeks and a mop of curly hair, runs out to draw the bolt on the teak gate and open it – a task which he performs with a speed and alacrity his father much admires. A bright, alert little boy he is and Mr Brand is justly proud of him. But now, as he looks in the car-mirror towards the gate behind him, he observes the boy begin to gesticulate, stabbing his forefinger in the direction of the back wheel. The look of alert brightness which he likes so much has been replaced by a look of fear, of panic almost; and this is compounded by the fact that, as well as gesticulating, the boy begins to shout. Having now reversed the car onto the roadway, Mr Brand jams on the brakes and lets the window down.

'What is it, Cornelius?' he calls testily, using the boy's full name. He does not encourage the 'Conny' his friends call him, an abbreviation not becoming for the son of a man of substance.

'It's the wheel, Daddy,' the boy tells him.

'What's wrong with it?'

'It's punctured. Flat.'

'Blast,' says Mr Brand, with injudicious candour. As a respected Director in the top managerial class, he demands high standards of himself and those around him. 'Blast' is not a word he would normally use.

Instantly, he is up and out of the car and around to the side where his son is standing. And there, as Cornelius had said, is the offending wheel, flat indeed as the proverbial pancake. What a vile let-down, he thinks: he, a man of standing, one who has taken the trouble of having a brand-new car every brand-new year, yet here it is, with not many days of that year spent, and already it has let him down.

For the second time that day, he is tempted to curse, to call heaven and earth down upon cars and car salesmen and all such false deceivers; to curse especially on this good morning his own bad luck; but that is not a thing a man such as he is may do. He was bred to better things and what breeding lacked his personal sense of order supplied. Besides, his little boy is standing there listening, others about the place may be listening too; he must not give bad example. This will be a tough job, a dirty job requiring much patience, so early in the morning too.

Well, so be it. That is what self-control and self-discipline are all about. On no account must he give in to outbursts of rage and bad temper. With the proper approach, it is the kind of situation which brings out the best in a man, and shows the difference between him and the common sort. Just keep cool, no panic, no complaint, put up with the stress of it, get on with the job. That is how difficult situations are handled, how the trials and tribulations in the life of a man of substance are overcome.

He takes off his driving gloves and car coat and, placing a car mat on the ground beside the wheel, goes down on his knees and sets to work. First, the jack and tool kit are removed from their brand-new casing; then, with the hubcap prised off, the jack is put in place and the brace fixed on the first of the wheel nuts. All this is done in due order, and will show his young son how to handle things when he grows up and the same happens to him; how, when life goes wrong, he must take it on the chin and face it. It will also show him that, though his father is a high-up, respected person in the world of business, he can also turn his hand to a tough task and hold his own with the best of them.

'It's important, Cornelius, for you to learn things like this,' he tells him. 'When you're a man, you'll have to face tough jobs, so don't be afraid of them. It's tests like this that make a man of you.'

The boy looks and listens. He much admires his father, as small boys do; now more than ever, seeing him go about this strange and difficult task with such apparent confidence.

But soon he begins to notice a change. The pace slackens, his father's talk stops, his breathing gets heavier and heavier. Worse still, words that sound very like 'Blast' and worse begin to reach his ears.

'I'm a bit out of practice at this,' he hears his father say; and then: 'I'm not as fit as I thought I was.' Through these scattered remarks, each time the man applies his strength to the brace and car jack, the going seems to get rougher; each time, failing to stir the tightened bolts, the curse-words get louder and more explicit. Still, knowing that his son is there beside him, he stays stubbornly at it, hoping that, sooner or later, it will work for him. It does not. At last, the jack locks at a point where the full weight of the car is on it; whereupon poor, sweating, exhausted Mr Brand – man of substance and exalted Director though he be – emits one final violent curse word and gives up.

It is at this juncture that fortune comes to his aid, in the form of a tanker bringing heating oil to one of the bungalows nearby. It pulls up in front of him and the driver gets out, leaving his helper to hook up the pipe for the delivery. With a sudden sense of relief, Mr Brand realises that he knows the man: a fine-looking young fellow he has seen in the public bar of the local hostelry on the odd occasion when, after a long directorial day, he passes through on his way to the lounge for a drink. He is glad of the acquaintance now: though by no stretch of the imagination would he call the man a friend, the old saying 'a friend in need is a friend indeed' flashes through his mind. Because a friend is what he urgently needs now, preferably a good strong one.

'Fine morning,' he calls cheerily, as the young man walks towards him.

'Good morning to you, sir,' he hears in reply. 'You seem to be having a spot of bother with the wheel.'

'Bother is right. I was on my way to work and bringing the young chap here to school when this thing happened, Dreadful the way things happen when you least want them.'

The man is right beside him now, looking down at the hunkered figure of the exalted, and exhausted, Mr Brand. For a moment, it seems to that good gentleman that the fellow is going to do no more than that, just stand there idly with his hands in his pockets and stare

172

at him. That is often the way with such people – curious in an idle way, but rarely if ever willing to do anything effective about it. Expect nothing of them and you will not be disappointed!

So be it, he thinks, I shall not demean myself by asking him to help. A man of substance must never be seen to demean himself like that, especially with his young son watching.

'Let me have a go at that,' the young man surprises him. 'Sometimes, when the bolts are new, they can be twice as hard to shift. To save time, go around the back you and get the spare wheel out.'

Mr Brand obeys, something which is quite new for him. He is not the obeying sort, still less when it is a casual truck driver who is doing the commanding. But there are times when it is no small part of wisdom to know how much of an evil may be tolerated. This is one of them.

In the few seconds it takes him to go around behind and get the spare wheel out, the young man has the brace turning like a corkscrew and the wheels lifting clear off the ground. The boy standing beside him cannot help noticing the contrast between this and the earlier efforts of his father about the task: there is no grunting-and-groaning, no heaving-and-sweating, no strangulated curse-words coming his way at all. It is all plain sailing, the man working away steady and sure, with the brace and car jack, the nuts and bolts like mere playthings in his hands.

'The trick is to take these things nice and easy,' he says. 'Once you do that, the job does itself.'

The proof is there for all to see: the jack is up full, the wheels are clear off the ground, the nuts turn freely to his firm touch. Nothing is left but to put the spare in place and away they go.

'You might give me a hand with this,' the young man tells Mr Brand, as he rolls the wheel into position before hanging it onto the protruding bolts. Yet again, the newly-compliant Mr Brand obeys. He gets down on his knees beside the man and holds the spare in place while the nuts are put in place and screwed home. The boy thinks it odd to see his father like this, down on his hunkers beside the oil man – he a mere truck driver in grimy overalls, his father an exalted man in a pinstripe suit. Their hands touch, they rub shoulders with each other like a pair of old buddies side by side together, their separate breaths merging into one in the frosty morning air. Nothing his father has ever said to him has prepared him for this.

But soon the job is done and Mr Brand is once more restored to his proper directorial role.

'Many hands make light work,' he says, with what might well be mistaken for the ghost of a smile. Then, remembering his inherited good manners, he adds: 'Thanks for the help.'

'Thanks for nothing, sir,' the young man replies. 'I just happened to be passing and you looked like you might need a bit of a hand.' The man who 'looked like he might need a bit of a hand' is just about to proffer his hand in a handshake when he thinks better of it. He had noticed the rough and grimy paws that had put his wheel in place a moment before; how could a man of substance demean himself by shaking hands with someone like that?

Still, he feels that something is needed, some gesture or token that will express his gratitude. It should, however, be something that will let his young son see that the two men's positions are worlds apart and, whatever about the camaraderie and mateyness of a moment ago, those positions are now properly re-adjusted: that he, Mr Brand, is back where *he* should be, the master; and the other man where he should be, his servant. For what is he in truth, this truck driver, but a hired hand whom Mr Brand had been obliged to take on in a moment of difficulty? What you do with someone like that is what you do in any master-servant relationship – you pay him.

He takes the wallet from his pocket and, fingering a crisp five pound note, hands it to the young man.

'Have a drink on this in the bar when you're next in,' he tells him. 'Who knows, if I see you on my way through to the lounge, I may even join you.'

The truck driver looks at the proffered note and at the genteel hand that proffers it. For the first time since he came upon this scene, his genial face begins to darken.

'No, thank you,' he says. 'I'd like to think I was doing a turn for a friend.'

The Reunion

Last of all in that little old cul-de-sac of ours was Clem Morgan. A crusty old devil he was, all by himself alone down there at the foot of the hill. He had a small pension from the flour mill where he had worked his way up from being a sack lifter to a supervisor, a pension which kept him in the frugal comfort which he had practised all his life. For such extras as he might need, he relied on the regular handouts which came to him from the only people in the world he cared about, his two brothers who had emigrated a long time ago and lived now on the Pacific coast of the United States.

Whenever they came home, as they did dutifully every three or four years, old Clem had a ball, living it up in style with them around the country, a big hired car under them, stopping off in grade A hotels, wining and dining in the best restaurants.

On the last occasion it happened the time seemed to fly; the weeks passed quicker than ever they did before; and, when the time came for them to leave, he stood with them in the departures lounge of Dublin Airport feeling indescribably sad. All he could think of were the thousands of miles that would stretch now between him and them – George in Los Angeles, Frank in San Francisco; of how they were getting old and this might very well be the last time he would see them. Little did he think that, within a few short months, it would turn out to be true. Frank was the first to go, slipping from a stepladder on the deck outside his penthouse suite onto the tiled patio below. When his wife came upon him several hours later, there he was, face upwards and smiling, but with his neck broken and his body gone stone cold.

That was a bad shock, which could not but have damaged George who, though some years younger, had had a heart problem all along. So, in a way, it came as less of a surprise to old Clem when he had a call from Los Angeles one night to say that he had had a massive coronary when walking upstairs to his Rodeo Drive office and had died in the ambulance on his way to hospital.

Clem was devastated by the double shock. Every moment of that last holiday with them came back to him, every stick and stone in the house they had touched while they were there came painfully alive. Though never much given to sentiment, he just sat there and cried. For a time, he even wished that he too could die, so as to be with them and have that happy month-long reunion with them go on forever. But that was an idle wish, it could never be so now.

In the morning when he woke, he was instantly conscious of this leaden weight pressing on him; at night, when he went to bed, he would lie there for hours, wishing, praying even, that, when he did get to sleep, he would not wake up. But the weeks passed, spring to summer, summer to autumn, and gradually, with the passing time, the sense of loss began to ease. He went about a bit more, read a little, looked at the news on his blotchy old television set. Tuesdays and Fridays he went to the Senior

Citizens Club where he played bridge with a few cronies older than himself, who spent their time grumbling about problems with pensions and medical cards. To the casual observer, this might have seemed like a return to normality, an acceptance of his brothers' deaths as the common lot of man; and, with that, a resolve to get on with his own life without them. And, in truth, in a way that is how it was. But, with that resignation had come a strange new feeling, a feeling he could not understand.

If he were a less thoughtful man, he might have paid less heed to it. If he were a man given to moods and mysteries; if his faith in the hereafter were strong; if he were forgetful, absent-minded, a daydreamer – if he were any of these things but what he was, a down to earth, solid, practical-minded person – he might have put it down to his imagination and thought no more about it. But he was none of those things and could not explain it in that way. The more he tried to explain it, the less explanation came; the more he tried to stifle and suppress it, the more it began to grow.

What he felt was that he was being – watched. Sometimes, when he was out for a walk, loping along in his lanky foxtrot, whatever it was that was watching him would seem to come closer. At times like that, he would pull the coat-collar up about his throat and trot a little faster to drive it away. It would not go away. What was it? Who was it? Why was it now steadily taking such a hold on his life? The moment he began to ask these questions, it would begin to fade. But no sooner would he think it gone than it would be back again, this time closer, more menacing, holding him in the grip of an unspoken, icy fear.

Then, one day in the Senior Citizens Club, he picked up a newspaper and his eye fell randomly on the column 'Your Luck With The Stars'. Under the heading 'Sagittarius', his star, he read the following:

'Today will bring new meaning to your life. It will begin a train of events which will culminate in a reunion with dear ones you have lost by the end of the year.'

His eyes lifted from the paper and whatever it was that was watching him seemed to draw closer. 'A reunion with dear ones you have lost'? How could that be? They were dead, how could he have a reunion with them? And 'by the end of the year'? That was but a few short months away. He tried to ignore the thing but could not. Instead, he took a nail scissors from his pocket and snipped it out. Then, putting it in his wallet, he went off home. But, no sooner was he in the door than a flight of starlings landed on the hawthorn bushes outside the window, making a great chirping and fluttering sound; and, when he went to look, what he saw in the glass was the reflection of his face, a face haunted by this new sense of foreboding. He took the newspaper cutting from his wallet and read it again. 'A reunion with dear ones you have lost . . . by the end of the year'. There was no doubt about it, that was what it said alright.

Why could he not have ignored it, turned the page and got on with the rest of the day's news? What was it but a snippet of print put together by some busybody with nothing better to do with his life? But he did not ignore it, he read it and kept it and, in the days and nights that followed, he read it again and again. There it was now on the table beside his bed, luring him, tempting him until, gradually at first, then more markedly, it began to assume a central place in his life.

There had been a time not long before when he thought he might have welcomed death, the only way he could hope to be reunited with his brothers who were gone; now, he began to dread it. He would grab at his pulse when he thought no one was looking and, failing to find it, would dig frantically at his wrist until it came. Had it begun to grow faint? Could that be his heart? Like his brother George? George had been the healthy one among them all their young lives, yet there he was, dead suddenly in an ambulance on his way to the hospital.

He would go to the mirror then and look at the face that confronted him. A grey, haggard face it had become, the face of a man who might indeed be about to . . . He dared not say the word. Why should dying have anything to do with him? He hadn't been sick, hadn't been to see a doctor in years. What a fool he was to be taken in by a silly old horoscope! Put it clean out of your mind, he told himself, forget it as if it had never been.

But, as he turned away from the mirror, he caught sight of the strange tint on his lips, a kind of purple tint, the same as George's had on the day he saw him off at Dublin Airport. He remembered too that, as they shook hands, George's hands were trembling, as his were trembling now.

The paper clipping on the bedside table seemed to curl up and leer at him. 'A reunion with dear ones you have lost . . . by the end of the year'. Much as he wanted to, he could not bring himself to tear it up there and then and throw it away, it had come to have such a deadly grip on his life.

Within a month, he had taken to the bed and the doctor was called. He couldn't eat, old Clem told him, nor could he sleep. Yet, when he was told that there was nothing the matter with him, so far as the doctor could see, he looked puzzled and did not seem to understand. He kept on repeating the same thing over and over: he hadn't eaten because he had no mind to eat; he couldn't sleep because he had strange dreams. What dreams, the doctor asked? He dreamed, he said, that he was going to die.

'Of course you're going to die,' he was told. 'We all are, there's nothing new in that. But that doesn't mean you have to do it before your time. It'll come soon enough, it will be time to think about it then.'

All the while this was going on, the doctor noticed that his eyes were fixed on the bedside table, where there was some cash, a few books and a small travelling clock; and, under the clock, held down by one of its legs, what appeared to be a newspaper cutting.

'Your horoscope,' the doctor quipped, picking it up and glancing at it. 'I hope it brings you good news!'

Weeks passed, the winter nights came down; soon the dark days coming up to Christmas were upon him. Still, he lay there, eating little, sleeping fitfully, waking with a start for fear he might be caught unawares. In the darkness, when he turned to see the time on the clock, the clipping under its leg would seem to move. He would force himself to turn away from it then, pull the bedclothes over his head, pretend it was not there. At last, worn out from waiting and watching, he would drop off; but, long before the first light seeped through the drawn blinds, the menacing words would come creeping back through his dozing brain: 'A reunion with dear ones . . . by the end of the year'.

Then, at last, it was New Year's Eve. When darkness fell, he dozed a while and, when he awoke, it was to hear what seemed like the sound of voices. He sat up in haste and looked about him – but there was nothing or no one there. Still, the voices kept coming, they would not go away. Off over in the far corner, the mahogany wardrobe bulked huge and fantastic in the gloom; nearby, the bedposts stood like leaden maces above his head. An icy wind whistled through the cracks in the windows and swept about the darkened room, carrying with it an echo of those menacing words.

His heart was pounding, the breath caught and tightened in his throat. He tried to raise himself on the pillow but could not. All he could do was to reach out to the bedside table towards the clipping under the clock's leg.

He grabs it and begins to crush, his arthritic fingers closing on it like claws, choking the life out of it and forcing it to silence. For it was from there that the voices were coming. At last, as he squeezes it into a tiny ball, up from the harbour through the thin night air comes the sound of ships' hooters bringing in the New Year. Five minutes to midnight, then he will be safe.

The breath still stuck in his throat; is it going to choke him? He holds on, each frantic gasp bringing him closer to the sound of the New Year bells.

He begins to count, the numbers coming to him in time with the ticking clock . . . 'One-two-three-four-five' . . . 'One-two-three-four' . . . 'One-two-three' . . . 'One-two' . . . 'One-'

The crushed paper slips from his fingers and falls to the ground. From out of the hollow darkness comes the sound of the New Year bells.